"I want you to say it, Isabella."

The devouring note in his voice and the look in his eyes had her heart ramming against her ribs as if unable to bear the confinement.

"I want you to say you've craved reclaiming what we had. That every time you closed your eyes, I was there, in your mind, on your tongue, all over you and inside you, giving you everything only I could ever give you."

Every word he said, soaked in hunger, seething with demand, brought a wave of wet heat surging in her core, her body readying itself for its master doing all the things she'd yearned for, as he'd said, for years, during every moment she had to herself.

Yet she still had to resist. Because of what he'd done to her in the past. And now.

* * *

Claiming His Secret Son
is part of The Billionaires of Black Castle series:
Only their dark pasts could lead these men
to the light of true love.

Dear Reader,

The Billionaires of Black Castle has been a rollercoaster ride for me to write. It was such a delight to explore the complex backgrounds, lives and psyches of this brotherhood of extraordinary men, who'd been taken by the malevolent Organization from childhood to exploit their outstanding abilities and turn them into unstoppable mercenaries.

But all through the first three books, the hero of *Claiming His Secret Son*, Richard Graves, was the most mysterious one of all. For the Englishman wasn't one of the brotherhood, but rather one of their jailers. Even after years of being the brothers' partner and the one who was responsible for their security, he remained an outsider. For everyone owed their allegiance to their leader, Numair Al Aswad, and Numair hated Richard irrevocably. In Numair's book, *Pregnant by the Sheikh*, we learned that Richard had transgressed unforgivably against Numair, betraying their friendship in the most heinous way.

So it was a great pleasure to be there while Richard told me his story, and why he'd become seemingly heartless and irredeemable. My pleasure intensified when Isabella exploded back into his life and started unraveling him. The son he discovered she'd borne him completed his undoing. There's nothing better than seeing such an all-powerful man brought to his knees by his love for his woman and child.

I so hope you enjoy reading his story as much as I enjoyed writing it.

I love to hear from readers, so please visit my website for my latest news at oliviagates.com, email me at oliviagates@gmail.com, and connect with me on Facebook, facebook.com/oliviagatesauthor, on Goodreads, goodreads.com/author/show/405461.Olivia_Gates and on Twitter, @OliviaGates.

Thanks for reading!

Olivia

CLAIMING HIS SECRET SON

OLIVIA GATES

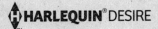

Recycling programs
for this product may
not exist in your area.

ISBN-13: 978-0-373-73400-9

Claiming His Secret Son

Copyright © 2015 by Olivia Gates

This edition published by arrangement with Harlequin Books S.A.

For questions and comments about the quality of this book, please contact us at CustomerService@Harlequin.com.

® and TM are trademarks of Harlequin Enterprises Limited or its corporate affiliates. Trademarks indicated with ® are registered in the United States Patent and Trademark Office, the Canadian Intellectual Property Office and in other countries.

Printed in U.S.A.

Olivia Gates has always pursued creative passions such as singing and handicrafts. She still does, but only one of her passions grew gratifying enough, consuming enough, to become an ongoing career—writing.

She is most fulfilled when she is creating worlds and conflicts for her characters, then exploring and untangling them bit by bit, sharing her protagonists' every heart-wrenching heartache and hope, their every heart-pounding doubt and trial, until she leads them to an indisputably earned and gloriously satisfying happy ending.

When she's not writing, she is a doctor, a wife to her own alpha male, and a mother to one brilliant girl and one demanding Angora cat. Visit Olivia at oliviagates.com.

Books by Olivia Gates

HARLEQUIN DESIRE

The Billionaires of Black Castle

From Enemy's Daughter to Expectant Bride
Scandalously Expecting His Child
Pregnant by the Sheikh
Claiming His Secret Son

Desert Knights

The Sheikh's Redemption
The Sheikh's Claim
The Sheikh's Destiny

Married by Royal Decree

Temporarily His Princess
Conveniently His Princess
Seducing His Princess

Visit the Author Profile page at Harlequin.com,
or oliviagates.com, for more titles.

To the romance writing community—
editors, authors, reviewers and readers—who
helped me realize not one but two major life goals.
This one is for you. Love you all.

One

Richard Graves adjusted his electric recliner, sipped a mouthful of straight bourbon and hit Pause.

The image on the hundred-plus-inch TV screen stilled, eliminating the unsteadiness of the recording. Murdock, his second-in-command, had taken the footage while following his quarry on foot. The quality was expectedly unsatisfactory, but the frame he'd paused was clear enough to bring a smile to his lips.

The only time a smile touched his lips, or he experienced emotions of any sort, was when he looked at her. At that graceful figure and energetic step, that animated face and streaming raven hair. At least, he guessed they were emotions. He had no frame of reference. Not in the past quarter of a century.

What he remembered feeling in his youth was so distant, it was as if he'd heard about it from someone else. Which was accurate. The boy he'd been before he'd joined The Organization—the criminal cartel that abducted and imprisoned children and turned them into unstoppable mercenaries—though as tough as nails, still held no resemblance to the invulnerable bastard everyone believed him—rightfully so—to be.

From what he remembered before his metamorphosis, and even after it, the most he'd felt had been allegiance, protectiveness, responsibility. For his best-friend-turned-nemesis Numair, for his disciple-turned-ally Rafael and to varying degrees for the Black Castle blokes—his reluctant partners in their globe-spanning business empire, Black Castle Enterprises—and their own. But that was where he drew the line in noble sentiments. What came naturally to him were dark, extreme, vicious ones. Power lust, vengeance, mercilessness.

So it never failed to stun him when beholding her provoked something he'd believed himself incapable of feeling. What he could only diagnose as…tenderness. He'd been feeling it regularly since he'd upgraded his daily ritual of reading surveillance reports on her to watching footage of what Murdock thought were relevant parts of her day.

Anyone, starting with her, would be horrified to learn he'd been keeping her under a microscope for years. And interfering in her life however he saw fit, undetectably changing the dynamics of the world she inhabited. He broke a dozen laws on a daily basis, from breach of privacy to coercion to…far worse, in his ongoing mission of being her guardian demon. Not that this was even a concern. The law existed for him to either break…or wield as a weapon.

But he *was* concerned she'd ever sense his surveillance or suspect his interference. Even if she never suspected it was him behind it all.

After all, she didn't even know he was alive.

As far as she knew he'd been lost since she was six. He doubted she even remembered him. Even if she did, it was best for her to continue thinking him gone, too.

Like the rest of their family.

So he only watched over her. As he had since she was born. At least, he'd tried to. There'd been years when he'd been powerless to protect her. But the moment he could, he'd given her a second chance for a safe and normal existence.

He sighed as he froze another image. He vividly remembered the day his parents had brought her home. Such a tiny, helpless creature. He'd been the one to give her her name. His little Rose.

She wasn't little now and certainly not helpless, but a surgeon, a wife, a mother and a social activist. He might help her here and there, but her achievements had all been ones of merit. He just made sure she got what she worked so hard for and abundantly deserved.

Now she had a successful career, a vocation and a husband who adored her—one he'd thoroughly vetted before letting him near her—and two children. Her family was picture-perfect, and not only on the outside.

Unfreezing the video, he huffed and tossed back the last of the bourbon. If only the Black Castle lads knew that he, aka Cobra, the most lethal operative The Organization had ever known and who was now responsible for their collective security, spent his evenings watching the sister they didn't know existed, who didn't know *he* existed, go about her very normal life. He'd never hear the end of it.

Suddenly he frowned, realizing something.

This footage didn't make sense. Rose was entering her and her husband's new private practice in Lower Manhattan. Murdock always only included new developments, emergencies or anything else that was out of the ordinary.

So watching Rose *was* his only source of enjoyment. But when he'd told Murdock to provide samples of Rose's normal activities, he'd stared emptily at him then continued to provide him only with what he considered worth seeing.

Had Murdock now decided to heed him and start giving him snippets of Rose walking down the street or shopping or picking her children up from school?

He snorted. That Vulcan would never do anything he didn't consider logical or pertinent. Even if he obeyed him blindly otherwise, Murdock wouldn't fulfill a demand he considered to be fueled by pointless sentiment and a waste of both their time.

This meant there was more to what he was watching than Rose entering her workplace.

What was he missing here?

Suddenly his heart seemed to hit Pause itself. Everything inside him followed suit, coming to a juddering standstill.

The person who entered the frame, the one Rose turned to talk to in such delight... Though the image was still from the back with only a hint of a profile apparent, he'd know that shape, that...*being*...blindfolded in a crowd of a million.

Her.

Sitting up, exercising the same caution he'd approached armed bombs with, he reached to the side table, vaguely noting how the glass rattled as he set it down. It wasn't his hand that shook. It was his heart. The heart that never crossed sixty beats per minute even under extreme duress. It now exploded from its momentary cessation in thunderclaps, sending recoil jolting through every artery and nerve.

The once waist-length, golden hair was now a dark, shoulder-length curtain. The body once rife with dangerous curves was svelte and athletic in a prim skirt suit. But there wasn't the slightest doubt in his mind. That *was* her.

Isabella.

The woman he'd once craved with a force that had threatened the fulfillment of his lifelong obsession.

He'd long resolved it according to his meticulous plan. It was *her* issue that hadn't been concluded satisfactorily. Or at all. She'd been his one feebleness, remained his only failure. The only one who'd made him swerve from his course and at times forget all about it. She remained the only woman he'd been unable—*unwilling* to use. But he'd let her use him. After their incendiary fling, when a choice had had to be made, she'd told him he'd never been an option.

Not that the memory of his one lapse was what had set off this detonation of aggression.

It was who she was. *What* she was.

The wife of the man who'd been responsible for the deaths of his family and for orphaning Rose.

He'd gone after her almost nine years ago as her husband's only Achilles' heel. But nothing had gone according to plan.

Her impact had been unprecedented. And it had had nothing to do with her rare beauty. Beauty never turned a hair on his head. Desire was his weapon, never his weakness. He'd been the one The Organization sent when women were involved, to seduce, use, then discard with utmost coldness.

But she'd been an enigma. At once clearly reveling in being the wife of a brute forty years her senior, who doted on her and submerged her in luxuries, while studying to be a doctor and involving herself in many humanitarian activities.

Going in, he'd been convinced her benevolent facade had been designed to launder her husband's image, in which she'd been succeeding, spectacularly.

But after he'd been exposed to her, this twenty-four-year-old who seemed much older than her years, he'd no longer been sure of anything. Seducing her had also proved much harder than he'd anticipated.

Though he'd been certain she'd reciprocated his unstoppable desire, she wouldn't let him near. Thinking she'd been only whetting his appetite until he was ready to do anything for a taste of her, as her husband had been, he'd intensified his pursuit. But it had only been after he'd followed her on a relief mission in Colombia—saving her and her companions during a guerilla attack—that her resistance had finally crumbled. The following four months had been the most delirious experience of his life.

He'd had to force himself to remember who she was to continue his mission. But it had been the hardest thing he'd ever done. When he'd had her in his arms, when he'd been inside her, he'd forgotten who he was.

But he'd finally extracted secrets only she'd known about her husband without her realizing it. Then he'd been ready to make his move. Not that it had been that easy.

Putting his plan into action had meant the end of his mission. The end of them. And he'd been unable to stomach walking away from her. He'd wanted more of her. Limitlessly more.

So he'd done what he'd never thought he'd do. He'd asked her to leave with him.

Though she'd claimed she couldn't think of life without him, her rejection had been instantaneous. And final. She'd never considered leaving her husband for him.

In his fever for a continuation of the affair, he'd convinced himself she'd refused because she feared her husband. So he'd pledged carte blanche of his protection.

But playing the distraught lover seamlessly, she'd still refused, adamant that there was no other way.

It had been only then that the red heat of coveting had hardened into the cold steel of cynicism. And he'd faced the truth.

She'd preferred her protection and luxury from the less-demanding man she'd married when she'd been twenty and had wrapped around her finger. Him, she'd only replace in her bed. There'd never been any reason she'd choose him over her decades-older ogre.

But he was certain she'd long regretted her choice when he'd shortly afterward destroyed her sugar daddy, protractedly, agonizingly, pulverizing her own life of excess with him.

Not that he'd cared what had happened to her. She'd made her bed of thorns thinking it was the lap of eternal luxury. It was only fitting she'd be torn apart lying in it.

But this searing vision from his past looked patently whole. Even in the video's inferior quality, he could sense her sangfroid. None of the hardships she must have suffered had come close to touching her.

Then it was over. The two women entered the building, and the video came to an abrupt end.

He stared at the black screen, questions an erupting geyser.

What was she doing at Rose's practice? This didn't seem to be a first-time meeting. So how had he missed the earlier ones leading to this level of familiarity? How had she come in touch with Rose at all?

This couldn't be a coincidence.

But what else could it be? There was no way she could know of his connection to Rose. His Richard Graves persona—the one he'd adopted after he'd left his Cobra days behind—had been meticulously manufactured. Not even The Organization with its limitless intelligence resources had found a shred of evidence tying him to their vanished agent.

Even if she'd somehow discovered the relationship between him and Rose, their affair had ended in unequivocal finality. No thanks to his own resolve. While he'd sworn he'd never check on her, he'd weakened on another front. He'd left the door ajar for a year afterward, in case she'd wanted to reestablish contact. Which she hadn't. If she'd wanted to do so now, she would have found a way to bring herself to his attention. It didn't make sense she'd target Rose to get to him. Or did it?

He exploded to his feet, snatched his phone out and punched Murdock's speed-dial number.

The moment the line opened, he barked, "Talk to me."

After a moment Murdock's deep voice was at once composed and surprised. "Sir?"

Impatience almost boiled his blood. "The woman with my sister. What was she doing with her?"

"It's all in the report, sir."

"Bloody hell, Murdock, I'm not reading your thirty-page report."

Silence greeted his snarl this time. Murdock must be stunned, since that was exactly what Richard had been doing for the past year. Murdock's documentation of Rose's every breath had been getting more extensive at his own demand. But right now he couldn't focus on a single paragraph.

"Everything I found out about Dr. Anderson's liaison with the woman in question is in the last two pages, sir."

"Did you sustain a serious head injury lately, Murdock? Am I not talking the Queen's English? I'm not reading two damned words. I want your verbal report. *Now.*"

At his barrage the man's chagrin almost crackled down the line, reminding him again that Owen Murdock was a relic of a bygone era.

Richard had always thought he'd be more at home in something like King Arthur's round table. He did treat Richard with the fervor of a knight in the service of his liege.

He'd been the first boy Richard had been given to train when he'd first joined The Organization as a handler...six years old to his own sixteen, making Murdock Rafael's age. He'd had him for six more years before Murdock had been taken from him and Rafael given to him instead.

Murdock had refused to accept anyone else's leadership, until Richard had been summoned to straighten him out. Richard had only told him to play along, that one day he'd get him out. Murdock had unquestioningly obeyed him. And believed him.

Richard had fulfilled his pledge, taking him away with him when he'd left, manufacturing a new identity for him, too. But instead of striking out on his own, Murdock had insisted on remaining in his service, claiming his training hadn't been complete. He'd actually been on par with the rest of the Black Castle chaps from day one, could have become a mogul in his own right, too. But Murdock had only wished to repay what he considered his debt to Richard before he could move on. Knowing how vital that had been to him, Richard had let him.

Now, ten years later, Murdock showed no signs of moving on. He'd have to shove him off the ledge soon, no matter if it would be like losing his right arm for real.

Murdock's current silence made Richard regret his outburst more. His number two prided himself on always anticipating his needs and surpassing his expectations. The last thing he wanted was to abuse such loyalty.

Before he made a retraction, Murdock talked, his tone betraying no resentment or mortification.

"Very well. At first, that woman appeared to be just another colleague of Dr. Anderson's. I ran a check on her, as I always do, and found nothing of note. But a development made me dig deeper. I discovered she'd changed her name legally five years ago, just before she made her first entry into the United States after a six-year hiatus. Her name was…"

"Isabella Burton."

Murdock digested the fact that Richard already knew her. He'd told neither him nor Rafael about the intensely personal mission he'd undertaken, or about her.

Murdock continued, "She's now Dr. Isabella Sandoval."

Sandoval. That wasn't either of her maiden names. Coming from Colombia, she'd had two. She must have been trying to become someone else when she'd adopted the new surname, after what had happened to her husband. That would also explain the changes in her appearance. And she *was* a doctor now.

Murdock went on, "But that wasn't what made me wary—what made me single out her meeting with Dr. Anderson to present to you. It's because I found a gaping thirteen-year hole in her history. From the age of twelve to the age of twenty-five, I couldn't find a shred of information on her."

Of course. She'd wiped clean the time she'd been Burton's wife, and for some reason only known to her, years before that. No doubt to hide more incriminating evidence that would prevent her from being accepted by any respect-ful society.

"The information trail starts when she was twenty-six, when she started a four-year surgical residency in Colombia, in affiliation with a pediatric surgery program in Califor-nia. It was a special 'out of the match' residency arrange-ment with the chief of surgery of a major teaching hospital. She obtained her US credentials and board certification last year. Then a week ago, she arrived in the United States and signed a one-year lease on a six-bedroom house in the For-est Hills Gardens section of Queens. She is here at the be-hest of doctors Rose and Jeffrey Anderson to start working in their private practice as a full partner, major shareholder and board member."

After that, Richard didn't know when he ended the call.

He only knew he was replaying that video over and over, Murdock's words a revolving loop in his mind.

Isabella. She was going to be his sister's partner.

Swearing under his breath, he almost cracked the remote in two as he pressed the off button.

Like hell she was.

Four hours later Richard felt as if the driver's seat of his Rolls Royce Phantom was sprouting red-hot needles.

It had been more than two hours since he'd parked across the street from his sister's house. He'd driven here immedi-ately when Murdock had called back saying he'd neglected to tell him Isabella was having dinner there tonight. She had yet to make an exit.

What was taking the bloody woman that long? What kind of dinner lasted more than four hours?

This alone told him things were worse than he'd first thought. Isabella seemed to be a close friend of his sister's, not just a prospective partner. And though Murdock hadn't been able to pinpoint the events leading to this bizarre status quo, Richard was certain this wasn't an innocent friendship.

Not on Isabella's side. She always had an angle. And obtained her objectives through deception and manipulation. Her medical qualifications themselves had probably been obtained through some meticulously constructed fraud.

Yet that was all conjecture. He had nothing solid to explain how Rose and her husband had developed such a deep connection with her that they'd invite her to be their equal partner in their life's crowning achievement. She'd made herself so invisible, her past so untraceable she'd fallen off Murdock's radar until now, when she was about to be fully lodged into their lives.

He'd torn over here once Murdock had informed him they'd finished dinner and coffee, expecting to intercept her soon afterward as she left. That had been—he flicked a glance at his watch—two and a half bloody hours ago.

Every minute of those he'd struggled with the urge to storm inside and drag her out.

He hadn't stayed out of his sister's life only to let that siren infect it with the ugliness of her past, the malice of her intentions and the exploitation in her blood.

Suddenly the front door of Rose's two-level, stucco house opened and two figures walked out. Isabella first, then Rose. His every muscle tensing, he strained to decipher the merriness that carried on the summer night air through his open window. Then they kissed and hugged and Isabella descended the stairs. At the bottom she turned to wave to Rose, urging her to go in, before she turned and crossed the street, heading to her car.

The moment Rose closed her door he got down from his car.

In the dim streetlights, Isabella's figure seemed to glow in a light-colored summer coat unbuttoned over a lighter dress beneath, its supple material undulating with her brisk walk. Her hair was a swathe of dark silk swinging over her face, her eyes downcast as she rummaged through her purse.

Then feet before he intercepted her, he stopped.

"Well, well, if it isn't Isabella Burton."

Her momentum came to a startled halt, her alarm a sharp gasp that echoed in the night's still, humid silence. Then her face jerked up and her eyes slammed into his.

A bolt struck him through the heart.

His sudden appearance seemed to have hit her even harder. If a ghost had stopped her to ask her the time, she wouldn't have looked more shocked...or horrified.

"What...where the hell did you...?"

She stopped. As if she found no words. Or breath with which to say them. He was almost as shocked as she was... at his reaction. He'd thought he'd feel nothing at the sight of her. He didn't know what he did feel now. But it was... enormous.

And it wasn't an overwhelming sense of familiarity. It was her impact as she was now.

She'd changed. Almost beyond recognition. It made it that much stranger he'd recognized her in that video so instantaneously. For this woman had very little in common with the younger one he'd known in total, tempestuous intimacy.

Her face had lost all the plumpness of youth, had been chiseled into a masterpiece of refinement and uncompromising character. If she'd been irresistible before, even with shock still seizing her every feature, the influence she'd exuded had matured into something far more formidable.

But her eyes had changed the most. Those eyes that had haunted him, eyes he'd once thought had opened up into a magical realm, that of her being. They *looked* the same, glowing that unique emerald-topaz chameleon color. But apart from the familiar shape and hue, and beneath the shock, they were bottomless. Whatever lay inside her now was dark and fathomless. And far more hard-hitting for it.

Her lids swept down, severing the two-way hypnosis. Gritting his teeth at losing the contact, his own gaze lowered to sweep her body. Even through the loose clothes, it still had his every sense revving. Just being near her had always made him ache.

Then a puff of breeze had her scent inundating him and his body flooded with molten steel. That was the one thing about her that hadn't changed. This distillation of her essence and femininity that had constantly hovered at the edge of his memory, tormenting him with craving the real thing.

And here it was at last. What he'd once thought an aphrodisiac nature had tailored to his senses. That belief was renewed in full force.

Hard all over, he returned his gaze to hers, eager to read her own response. She poured every bit of height and poise into her statuesque figure, made him feel she was looking him in at eye level when even in three-inch heels, she stood seven inches below his six-foot-six frame.

"Richard." She gave a formal nod as if greeting a virtual stranger. Then she just circumvented him and continued walking to her car.

He let her pass him, one eyebrow rising.

So. His opening strike hadn't been as effective as he'd planned. She'd gotten over her shock at seeing him faster than he had and had decided to dismiss him.

Surely she considered anyone who knew her real identity a threat to her carefully constructed new persona. But if there were levels of danger to blasts from the past, she must think his potential damage equivalent to a ballistic missile. She couldn't end this "chance" meeting fast enough.

Which proved she hadn't tied him to Rose, wasn't here because of anything concerning him. But that changed nothing.

Whatever she was here for, she wasn't getting it.

He stared ahead, listening to the steady staccato of her receding heels, a grim smile twisting his lips.

In the past he'd been the one who'd walked away. But it had been her who'd made the decision. It now entertained him to let her think the choice remained hers. He'd let her strike his presence up to coincidence, think it would cause no repercussions for her. Then he'd disabuse her of the notion.

Last time, he hadn't been able to override her will. This time, he'd make her do what he wanted. And right now, all he wanted was to taste her once more. He'd postpone his real purpose until he satisfied the hunger that had roared to life inside him again at the sight of her.

He'd much prefer it if she struggled, though.

The moment he heard her opening her car, he turned and sauntered toward her.

She lurched as he passed behind her and murmured, "I'll drive ahead. Follow me."

He felt her gaze boring into his back as he reached his car two spaces ahead. Opening his door, he turned around smoothly, just in time to witness her reaction.

"What the hell...?" She stopped, as if it hurt to talk.

He sighed. "My patience has already been expended for the night. Follow me. Now."

Her eyes blazed at him as she found her voice again. Not the velvety caress that had echoed in his head for eight endless years but a sharp blade. "I'll do no such thing."

"My demand was actually a courtesy. I was trying to give you a chance to preserve your dignity."

Her mouth dropped open. His own lips tingled.

Then his tongue stung when hers lashed him. "Gee, thanks. I can preserve it very well on my own. I'll drive away now, and if you follow me, I'll call the police."

Hostility was the last thing he'd predicted her reaction would be, considering the last time he'd seen her she'd wept as he'd walked away as if her heart were being dragged out of her body. But it only made his blood hurtle with vicious exhilaration. She was giving him the struggle he'd hoped for, the opportunity to force her to succumb to him this time. And he would make her satisfy his every whim.

He gave her the patented smile that made monsters quiver. "If you drive away, I won't follow you. I'll knock on your friends' door and tell them whom they're really getting into business with. I don't think the Andersons would relish knowing you were—and maybe still are—the wife of a drug lord, slave trader and international terrorist."

Two

Isabella stared up at the juggernaut that blocked out the world, every synapse in her brain short-circuiting.

When he'd materialized in front of her, like a huge chunk of night taking the form of her most hated entity, her heart had almost ruptured.

But she'd survived so many horrors, had always had so much to protect, her survival mechanisms were perpetually on red alert. After the initial brutal blow, they'd kicked in as she'd made an instinctive escape. That didn't mean she hadn't felt about to crumple to the ground with every breath.

Richard. Here. Out of the depths of the dark, sordid past. The man who'd seduced and used…and almost destroyed her.

That he hadn't succeeded hadn't been because he hadn't given it his best shot. Ever since, she'd been trying to mend the rifts he'd created in the very foundations of her being. She'd only succeeded in painting over the deepest ones. Though she now seemed whole and strong, those cracks had been worsening over time, and she was sure they'd fissured right to her soul.

But she'd just reached what would truly be a new start. Then he'd appeared out of thin air.

It had flabbergasted her even more because she'd just been thinking of him. It had been as if she'd conjured him.

Yet when had she ever stopped thinking of him? Her memory of him had been like a pervasive background noise that could never be silenced. A clamor that rose to a crescendo periodically before it settled back to a constant, maddening drone.

But there was one explanation for his reappearance. That it was a fluke. An appalling one, but one nonetheless. What else could it have been after eight years?

Not that time elapsed was even an issue. It could have been eight days and she would have thought the same thing. She'd long realized he'd left her believing he'd never see her again.

After all, he must have known what he'd done would most probably get her killed.

Believing their meeting to be a coincidence, she'd run off, thinking the man who'd once exploited her then left her to a terrible fate would shrug and continue on his way.

But just as she'd thought she'd escaped, that he'd fade into the night like some dreadful apparition, he'd followed her. Before she could deal with the dismay of thinking this ordeal would be prolonged, he'd made his preposterous demand.

Not that it had felt like one. It had felt like an ultimatum. Her instinct had been correct.

She hadn't forgiven him, nor would she ever forgive him, but she'd long rationalized his actions. From what she'd discovered—long after the fact—he obtained his objectives over anyone's dead body, figuratively or literally. She, and everything he'd done to her, had been part of a mission. She only had theories what that had been or why he'd undertaken it, according to the end result.

But what he was doing now, threatening with such patent enjoyment what he must know would destroy everything she'd struggled to build over the past eight years, was for his own entertainment. That man she'd once loved, with everything in her scarred psyche and starving soul, had progressed from a cold-bloodedly pragmatic bastard into a full-fledged monster.

"Don't look so horrified."

His bottomless baritone swamped her again, another thing about him that had become more hard-hitting. The years had turned the thirty-four-year-old demigod of sensuality she'd known into an outright god, if one of malice. He still exuded sex and exerted a compulsion—both now magnified by increased power and maturity. But it was this new malevolence that now seemed to define him. And it made him more overwhelming than ever.

But that must have been his true nature all along. It was she who'd been blinded and under his control. She hadn't even suspected what he'd been capable of long after he'd gotten everything he'd wanted from her, then tossed her to the wolf.

"I'm not interested in exposing you." His voice had her every hair standing on end. "As long as you comply, your secret can remain intact."

Summoning the opaqueness she'd developed as her greatest weapon against bullies such as him, she cocked her head.

"What makes you think I haven't told them everything?"

"I don't think. I know. You resorted to extreme measures to construct this St. Sandoval image. You'd go as far to preserve it. You'll certainly give in to anything I demand so no one, starting with the Andersons, ever finds out what you really are."

"*What* I am? You make it sound as if I'm some monster."

"You're married to one. It makes you the same species."

"I'm not married to Caleb Burton. I haven't been for eight years."

Something…scary slithered in the depths of his cold steel eyes. But when he spoke, he sounded as offhand as before.

"So it's in the past tense. A past full of crimes."

"I never had a criminal record."

"Your crimes remain the same even if you're not caught."

"What about your crimes? Let's talk about those."

"Let's not. It would take months to talk about those, as

they're countless. But they're also untraceable. But yours could be easily proved. You knew exactly how your husband made his mushrooming fortune and you made no effort to expose him, making you an accessory to his every crime. Not to mention that you helped yourself to millions of his blood money. Those two charges could still get you ten to fifteen years in a snug little cell in a maximum-security prison."

"Are you threatening to turn me in to the law, too?"

"Don't be daft. I don't resort to such mundane measures. I don't let the law take care of my enemies or chastise those who don't fall in line with my wishes. I have my own methods. Not that I have to resort to those in your case. Just a little chat with your upstanding friends and they wouldn't consider getting mixed up with someone with your past."

"Contrary to what you believe, from your own twisted self and life, there are ethical, benevolent people in the world. The Andersons don't hold people's pasts against them."

He gave her back her pitying disdain, raised her his own brand of annihilating taunting. "If you believed that, you wouldn't have gone to such painstaking lengths to give your history, and yourself, a total makeover."

"The makeover was only for protection, as I'm sure you, as the world's foremost mogul of security solutions, are in the best position to appreciate."

His lethal lips tugged. "Then, it won't matter if your partners in progress find out the details of your previous marriage to one of the world's most prominent figures in organized crime. Along with the open buffet of unlawful immorality that marriage entailed and that you buried. Refuse to follow me and we get to put your conviction of *their* convictions to the test."

Feeling the world emptying of the last atom of oxygen, she snapped, "What the hell do you want from me?"

"To catch up."

Her mouth dropped open.

It took effort to draw it back up, to hiss her disbelief. "So you see me walking down the street and decide on the spot to blackmail me because the urge to 'catch up' overwhelmed you?"

His painstakingly chiseled lips twisted, making her guts follow suit. "Don't tell me you thought it even a possibility I happened to be taking a stroll in a limbo of suburban domesticity called Pleasantville, of all names?"

"You were following me."

The instant certainty congealed her blood. Realizing his premeditation made it all so much worse. And the possible outcomes unthinkable.

He shrugged. "You took your time in there. I was about to knock on the Andersons' door anyway to see what was taking you so long."

Not putting anything beyond him, she imagined how much worse it would have been if he'd done that. "And you went to all this trouble to 'catch up'?"

"Yes. Among other things."

"What other things?"

"Things you'll find out when you stop wasting time and follow me. I'd tell you to leave your car, but your friend might see it and get all sorts of worrisome ideas."

"None would be as bad as what's really happening."

His expression hardened. She was sure it had brought powerful men to their knees. "Are you afraid of me?"

That possibility clearly hadn't occurred to him before. Now that it did, it seemed to…offend him.

The weirdest part was, though she'd long known he was a merciless terminator, her actual safety wasn't even a concern.

It was in every other way that she feared him.

She wasn't about to tell him that. But she did give him an honest answer to his query. "I'm not."

"Good."

His satisfaction chafed her. The urge to wipe it off his cruelly perfect face surged. "I'm not, because I know if you wanted to harm me, I wouldn't have known what hit me. That you're only coercing me indicates I'm not on your hit list."

"It is heartening that you grasp the situation." That soul-searing smile played on his lips again. "Shall we?"

She stood there, her gaze trapped in his, her thoughts tangling.

They both knew he'd cornered her from the first moment. But succumbing to this devil without resistance would have been too pathetic. She'd at least let loose some of her anger and bitterness toward him first. What she'd thought long extinguished.

It was clear they'd only been suppressed under layers of self-delusion so they wouldn't destroy whatever remained of her stability, what everything—and everyone—in her life depended on.

Now that she'd admitted that, it was easier to admit why she'd succumb to his coercion.

The first reason was that she would have, even without his threat. If he'd turned a consummate fiend like Burton into mincemeat so effortlessly when he'd been a younger and less powerful man, she didn't want to know what he was capable of now. She was nowhere in his league. No one was.

The second was harder to face. But what she'd belatedly learned about his truth and that of what they'd shared and what he'd done to her *had* left a gaping hole inside her.

She wanted that hole filled. She wanted closure.

Holding his hypnotic gaze, she finally nodded.

He just turned and walked away. Before he lowered himself into the gleaming black beast that looked as sleek, powerful and ruthless as he did, he tossed her an imperious glance over his acres-wide shoulders.

"Chivvy along."

At his command to hurry up in his native British English, she expelled the breath she'd been holding.

Chivvy along, indeed.

Might as well get this over with as quickly as possible.

In minutes she was following him as ordered as he headed to Manhattan, emotions seething inside her. Fury, frustration, fear—and something else.

That "something else" felt like…excitement.

How sick would that be? To be excited by the man who'd decimated her heart and almost her world, who'd just threatened to complete the job and had her following him like a puppy?

But…maybe not so sick. Excitement could encompass trepidation, anxiety, uncertainty. And everything with Richard had always contained maximum doses of all that. It was why he'd been the only one who'd made her feel…alive. She'd been in suspended animation before she'd met him and since he'd walked away.

For better, or in his case, for worse, it seemed he'd remain the only one who could reanimate her.

"Get it over with. Catch up."

Isabella threw her purse on the black-and-bronze Roberto Cavalli leather couch and looked at Richard across his gigantic, forty-foot-ceilinged, marble-floored reception area.

He only continued preparing their drinks at the bar, his lupine expression deepening.

So. He'd talk when he wished. And he hadn't wished. Yet. Got it.

Good thing she'd called home during the forty-minute drive to say she'd be *very* late.

Pretending to shrug away his disregard, she looked around. And was stunned all over again.

The Fifth Avenue penthouse overlooking the now shrouded in darkness Central Park and Manhattan's glittering Upper East Side drove home to her how staggeringly wealthy he was now. The opulent, technologically futuristic duplex on the sixty-seventh and sixty-eighth floors had to have cost tens of millions.

Among the jaw-dropping features of the fully automatic smart-home was its own elevator, its remote-, voice- and retinal-recognition doors and just about everything else.

It even housed a thirty-by-fifty-foot pool.

As they'd passed the sparkling expanse, he'd told her something she hadn't known about him. That he hated the sun and preferred indoor sports. She'd already worked out that he hated people, too. A pool in his living room at the top of the world away from the nuisance of mere mortals was a no-brainer to someone with his kind of money.

He'd been saying he'd expand the pool to get a decent exercise without having to flip over and over when she'd stopped listening. The image of him shooting through the liquid turquoise like a human torpedo, then rising from the water like an aquatic deity with rivulets weeping down his masterpiece body had tampered with her mental faculties.

Snatching her thoughts away before they slid back into *that* abyss, she examined the L-shaped terrace of at least five-thousand square feet. The city views must be breathtaking from there. They were from every corner in this marvel of a home.

Though *home* sounded so wrong. Anywhere he was could never be a home. This place felt like an ultramodern demon's den.

Avoiding looking at him, she noted the designer furniture and architectural touches that punctuated each zone, couldn't guess at many of the functional features. But it was spectacular how the mezzanine level took advantage of the massive ceiling heights and ingeniously provided extensive library shelves. He'd probably read every book. And archived its contents in that labyrinthine mind of his.

But what made the mezzanine truly unique was its glass floors and balustrade, with the staircase continuing the transparent theme. Looking down wouldn't be for the fainthearted.

But Richard didn't have to worry about that, since he was heartless. A fact this astounding but soulless place clearly underlined.

That he had other residences on the West Coast and in England, as he'd offhandedly informed her as they'd entered this place, no doubt on the same level of luxury and technology, was even more mind-boggling. Burton had been a billionaire and it had been hard to grasp the power such wealth brought. But those had been a fraction of Richard's, who was currently counted among the top one hundred richest men on the planet. The security business was booming, and his empire reigned over that domain.

But money, in his case, was the result of the immense influence of his personality and expertise, not the other way around. And then there were his connections. Black Castle Enterprises, which he'd built from the ground up with six other partners, had a major hand in everything that made the world go round and was one of the most influential businesses in history.

"I just learned of your presence in the country today."

His comment dragged her out of her musings, his deepened voice making the cultured precision of his British accent even more shiver worthy. She'd always thought that killer brogue of his the most evocative music. She used to ask him to speak just so she could revel in listening to him enunciate. It had always aroused the hell out of her, too.

But everything about him always had. During the four months of their affair she'd been in a perpetual fugue of arousal.

She watched him approach like a leisurely tiger stalking his kill, every muscle and sinew flexing and pulling at his fitted black shirt and pants, his stormy sky-hued eyes striking her with a million volts of charisma. The familiar ache she hadn't felt since she'd last seen him, that had been trembling under the suppression of shock, hostility and anxiety since he'd appeared before her, stirred in her deepest recesses.

Time had been criminally indulgent with him, enhancing his every asset—widening his shoulders, hardening his waist and hips, bulking up his torso and thighs. Age had taken a sharper chisel to his face, hewing it to dizzying planes and angles, turning his skin a darker copper, intensifying the luminescence of his eyes. His luxurious raven hair had been brushed with silver at the temples, adding the last touch of allure. He was now the full potential of premium manhood realized.

As he reached for the cocktail glass, his fingertips grazed hers, zapping her with a bolt of exquisite electricity.

Great. His deceit and her ignorance of his true nature and intentions had had nothing to do with his effect on her as she'd long told herself. He'd almost cost her her life, and she knew what he truly was and how she'd been a chess piece he'd played and disposed of…yet it made no difference to her body. It didn't deal in logic, cared nothing about dignity and hadn't learned a thing from the harsh lessons of experience. It only saw and sensed the man who'd once possessed and pleasured it almost beyond endurance.

She sat before he realized he still liquefied her knees… and everything else. When she'd thought she'd irreversibly turned to stone.

But she'd thought that before she'd first met him. It had taken him one glance to get the heart she'd believed long petrified quivering. He remained the one man who could reverse any protective metamorphosis.

Safe on a horizontal surface, she looked way, way up at him as he loomed over her like a mystic knight, or rather a malevolent wizard, from an Arthurian fairy tale.

"So the moment you realized I was on American soil, you decided to track me down and ambush me."

"Precisely."

In a heartbeat he was beside her. She marveled again at the strength and control needed for someone of his height and bulk to move so effortlessly. Even though he didn't come too near, her every nerve fired.

Sipping the amber liquid in his crystal glass, he turned to face her fully. "I've been remembering how we met."

She sipped her drink only to suppress the impulse to hurl it in his face. The moment it slid down her throat she realized how parched she was. And how it hit the spot. Perfect coolness and flavor, light on alcohol, heavy on sweetness.

He remembered. How she took her drinks.

Something suffocating, something similar to regret, swept her.

Suddenly the bitterness that had lain dormant in her depths seethed to the surface again. "We didn't meet, Richard. You tracked me down then, too. And set me up."

Nonchalance tugged a corner of his lips. "True."

She took another sip, channeling her anger into sarcasm. "Thanks for sparing me the aggravation of denial."

His gaze lengthened, becoming more unreadable and disturbing. Then he shrugged. "I don't waste time on pointless pursuits. I already realized you know everything. From the first moment, your hostile attitude made it clear I'm not talking to the woman who cried rivers at my departure."

"Why conclude that was because I *know everything*? That could have been classic feminine bitterness for said departure. Surely you didn't expect even the stupid goose I used to be to throw herself in your arms after eight years?"

"Time is irrelevant." Just what she'd been thinking. "It's what you realized that caused you to change. You clearly worked everything out." His gaze intensified, making her feel he was probing her to her cellular level. "So how did you?"

"You know how."

"I probably do. But I'd still like to know the actual details of how you came to realize the truth."

A mirthless laugh escaped her. "If you're asking so you never repeat whatever clued me in, don't bother. Working it all out wasn't due to any discernment on my side, and I only did over three years after the fact." One formidable eyebrow rose at that particular detail. "Yeah, pathetic, right?"

"Not the adjective I'd use." She waited for him to substitute his own evaluation, but he left her hanging. "I don't want details as a prophylactic measure for future operations. I know I am untraceable. Your deductions couldn't have been backed up by any evidence. Even if they were, I made sure your best interest remained in burying any."

"So you're asking only to marvel at how good you are?"

"I know exactly how good I am." The way he said that… The ache deep inside started to throb. "I don't need validations nor do I indulge in self-congratulations." Eyes narrowing, his focus sliced through her. "Why the reluctance to tell me? We're laying our cards down now that the game is long over."

"You laid down nothing."

"I'll lay down whatever you wish." When she opened her mouth to demand he start, he preempted her. "You first."

Knowing she'd end up giving him what he wanted, she sighed. "When the blows to Burton started coming out of the blue, I just thought he'd slipped in his secrecy measures. One day, when he was finally on his knees, he asserted that the breach hadn't come from his side, that I was the only one who knew everything he did. I thought he was just looking for someone to blame, but that didn't change a thing. I believed he'd soon make up his mind that I betrayed him. So I ran."

Draining his glass, he grimaced, set it down on the coffee table. Then he sat back, his eyes so intense it felt as if he was physically attempting to yank the rest out of her.

Torrents of accusations almost spilled from her. Forcing them down, she skipped over the two worst years of a generally hellish existence, and went on, "I only revisited his accusations *much* later, started to wonder if I'd been some-how indiscreet. That pointed me in the direction of the only one I could have been indiscreet with. You. That led to a reexamination of our time together, and to realizing your ingeniousness in milking me for information."

"And you realized it was I who sent him to hell."

She nodded, mute with the remembered agony of that awareness. She'd felt such utter betrayal, such total loss. Her will to go on, for a while, had been completely spent.

"It dawned on me that you had targeted me only to get my insider info and asked me to leave with you to agonize and humiliate him on every front. Everything made so much sense then I couldn't believe I didn't suspect you for years. Who else but you could have devised such a spectacular downfall for him? It takes a monster to bring down another."

His watchfulness lifted, fiendishness replacing it. "*Monster* wasn't what you screamed all those times in my bed."

"Don't be redundant. I already admitted I was too oblivi-ous to live. But once the fog of my obliviousness cleared, I only wished I could forget ever meeting you."

"Don't hold your breath. Even if our meeting wasn't spontaneous, it wasn't only memorable, it remains indel-ible."

The fateful encounter that had turned her life upside down had been that way for him, too?

His cover story had been arranging security for the hu-manitarian organization she'd been working with. He'd de-manded to meet all volunteers for a dangerous mission in Colombia to judge who should go.

Her first glimpse of him remained branded in her mind.

Nothing and no one had ever overwhelmed her as he had. And not because he'd been the most gorgeous male she'd ever seen. His influence far transcended that. His scrutiny had been denuding, his questions deconstructing. He'd rocked her to her core, making her feel like a swooning moron as she'd sluggishly answered his rapid-fire questions.

After telling her she'd passed his test, she'd exited his office reeling. She hadn't known it possible for a human being to be so beautiful, so overpowering. She hadn't known a man could have her hot and wet just by looking at her across a desk. She hadn't been interested in a man before, so the intensity of her desire for him, for his approval, and her delight at earning it had flung her in chaos. She'd never known such excitement, such joy...

"The changes become you."

She blinked, realized she'd been staring at him all the time. As he'd been staring at her.

"The sculpting of your body and features...the darkening of your hair. An effective disguise, but also an enhancement."

"I wanted to look different for security reasons, but ended up not needing to do anything. Time and what it brought did it all."

"You talk as if you're over the hill."

"I feel it. And that's my real hair color. No longer bleaching my hair was the second best thing I ever did, after getting rid of Burton himself, who insisted I looked better as a blonde."

His lips compressed. "Burton wasn't only a depraved wanker, but a gaudy maggot, too. The feast of caramels and chocolates of your hair pays tribute to your creamy complexion and jeweled eyes far better than any blond shade would, framing them to the best effect possible."

She blinked again. Richard Graves paying her a compliment? And such a flowery one, too?

And he wasn't finished. "Before I approached you, I had photos, knew of your unusual beauty. But when I saw you in the flesh, the total effect punched me in the gut and not just on account of your looks. Time had only scraped away whatever prettiness youth inflicted and brought you profound beauty in its place. I believe it will only keep bestowing more on you. You were stunning, but you've become exquisite. With age, you'll become divine."

She gaped at him. Once, when she'd believed him to be a human being, not a machine that made money and devised plans of annihilation, she'd believed him when he'd praised her beauty. But even then, when he'd been doing everything to keep her under his spell, he'd never done it with such fervor and poetry. That he did so now…offended her beyond words.

Fury tumbled in her blood. "Spare me the nausea. We both know what you really think of me. Is this one of the 'other things' you had in mind? To ply me with preposterous flattery and have some more sick fun at my expense?"

"I was actually trying my hand at sincerity." He turned fully to her. "As for the 'other things' I had in mind, it's… *this*."

And she found herself flat on her back with Richard on top of her, his chest crushing her breasts, his hips between her splayed thighs.

Before her heart could fire the next fractured beat, he rose over her and stopped it.

This was how a devil must look before he took one's soul.

Inescapable. Ravenous. Dreadfully beautiful.

"Eight years, Isabella. Eight years without this. Now I'll have it all again. I'll consume every last inch and drop of you. That's why I brought you here. And that's why you really came."

Three

Time congealed as she lay beneath Richard, paralyzed. Even her heart seemed afraid it would rupture if it beat.

Then everything that had been gathering inside her since he'd walked away—all the betrayal and despondence and yearning—broke through the cracks and she started to tremble.

A shudder traversed his great body as if her tremors had electrified him, making him crush her harder beneath him, crash his lips on her wide-open ones.

His tongue thrust deeply and his scent and taste flooded her bloodstream, a hit of a drug she'd gone mad for since she'd been forced to give it up cold turkey. Gulping it down, she rode rapids of mindlessness as he filled her, drank her the way she remembered and craved. Richard didn't kiss. He invaded, ravaged.

He didn't only catapult her into a frenzy, but sent her spiraling into a reenactment of that first kiss that had launched her addiction.

That day he'd materialized like an answer to a prayer, cutting down the guerillas who'd been threatening her team with death…or worse. She'd been so shaken thinking she could have died without having the one thing she'd ever wanted—him—had been so grateful, so awed, she'd gone to offer him what he'd seemed to want so relentlessly. Herself.

He'd let her into his room, his gaze consuming her, letting her see what he'd do to her once she gave him consent.

And she had, melting against him, giving him permission to do anything and everything to her.

He'd taken her mouth for the first time then, with that same thorough devouring, that coiled ferocity. From that moment on her body had learned what heart-stopping pleasure his kiss would lead to, had afterward burst into flames at his merest touch, the fire raging higher with each exposure.

The conflagration was fiercer now, with the fuel of anger and animosity, with the accumulation of pain and craving and repression. This was wrong, insane. And it only made her want it—want *him*—more than her next breath.

His roughness as he teased her turgid nipples, his dominance as he ground against her molten core, made her spread her thighs wider, strain to enfold him, her moans rising, blind arousal fracturing the shackles of hostility and memory, drowning them and her.

Suddenly he severed their meld, wrenching a cry of loss from her as he rose above her.

His gaze scalded her, his lips filled with grim sensuality. "I should have listened to my body—and yours—and done this the moment I got you in here."

His arrogance should have made her buck him off. But lust for this memorized yet unknown entity, so deadly and irresistible, seethed its demand for satisfaction.

"Say this is what you wanted all along. *Say* it, Isabella."

A hard thrust and squeeze of her buttocks accompanied his brusque order, melting her further. But it was the harshness on his face that jogged her heart out of its sluggish surrender.

The world spun with too many emotions, after years of stasis. Years when she'd felt him this way only in dreams that had always turned into nightmares. In those visions, he'd always aroused her to desperation before pushing her away and taking off his mask. The merciless face he'd exposed before walking over her sobbing body had always woken her in tears then plunged her into deeper despondence.

Dreading those nightmares had robbed her of the ability to rest. It was the memory of them now that made her struggle to stop her plummet into the abyss of addiction all over again.

"What if I don't say it?" Her voice shook.

At her challenge, his gaze emptied of intensity. He released her trembling flesh and in one of those impossible moves, he separated their bodies and was on his feet.

To her shame, she'd thought his response to her challenge would be to take his onslaught to the next level. She still expected he'd pick her up and carry her off to bed.

He only sat on the coffee table, clearly deciding to end their encounter. The letdown deepened her paralysis.

His brooding gaze made her acutely aware of how pathetic she looked prostrated as she was, sending chagrin surging through her numb limbs. Feeling she'd turned to jelly, she pulled herself up and her dress down.

Once she'd tidied the dishevelment he'd caused, he drawled, "Now that there's no hint of physical coercion... *say* it."

Her heart skidded at his deceptively calm command. "You mean there's no coercion because you're not on top of me anymore? I'm here *purely* by coercion."

"I submit, this is false. I only gave you an excuse to have your cake and eat it, too, a justification you can placate your dignity with. But it's easy to invalidate your self-exonerating assertion. I'll escort you to the door, activate it for you and you can walk right out."

"And then you'll call my friends."

"There *are* things you could do that would make me do that. None of them include choosing to walk out now." He rose to his feet. "Shall we?"

She scrambled to her feet only when she found him striding away for real and had to almost run in his wake.

"That's it? You go to all this trouble to get me here, interrogate me for a bit, then abruptly shift to what seems to be your real objective, and when I refuse to 'say it' you show me the door?"

"I have to. It won't open unless I tell it to."

His derision, and the fact that he'd shrugged off what had happened when it had turned her inside out had her fury sizzling.

Catching up with his endless strides beside the pool, she snatched at his arm. Her fingers only slipped off his rock-hard muscles. It was he who stopped of his own accord, daring to look as if he had no idea what was eating her, but was resigned to putting up with an inexplicably hysterical female.

"Why do you want me to say it?" she seethed. "Is your ego that distorted? You want me to admit how much I want you when you never wanted me in the first place?"

His winged eyebrow arched more. "I didn't?"

"If we're both certain of one thing, it's that."

"And you've come to that conclusion, how?"

"Like I did all the rest. Seduction is no doubt your weapon of choice with women, and pretending to desire me was only to turn me into your willing thrall. The info I had was my only real use to you."

He inclined his head as if examining a creature he'd never known existed. "You think I spent four months in bed with you and didn't desire you?"

"You're a man, and an overendowed one. I bet you could…perform with any reasonably attractive female, especially one in heat."

"That you were." His reminiscent look made her want to smack him across that smug mouth. "I never thought a woman could always be that hot and ready for me." Before she lashed out, he sighed. "I *would* have seduced you even if you'd been a slime-oozing monstrosity. Stomaching a mark was never a prerequisite in my search-and-seduce missions. But even based on my indiscriminate libido, as you presume, I would have still suffered the minimum of physical contact to keep you on the hook. I wouldn't have gone to lengths you can't imagine to create a rendezvous almost daily, and then to have sex with you as many times as could be squeezed into each encounter. Even with my 'endowments' I couldn't have *performed* that repeatedly or that…vigorously if I wasn't even hotter and readier for you than you were for me. And I was. None of that was an act."

Her heart stuttered as she met the gaze that suddenly felt as if it held no barriers. As if he was telling the truth, probably for the first time.

He'd really wanted her?

But… "If you wanted me as much as you claim, and still used and discarded me like any other woman you didn't want, that makes you an even colder bastard."

His gaze grew inscrutable again. "I didn't discard you. You chose Burton."

"Is that what you call what I did? I had no choice."

"You always have a choice."

"Spare me the human-development slogans."

"A choice doesn't have to be an easy one, but it remains one. Every choice has pros and cons. Once you make one, you put up with its consequences. You don't blame others for those."

"I categorically disagree. I certainly blame others, namely Burton and you, for making it impossible for me to have a choice. Leaving him was out of the question."

"You did end up leaving him."

"I didn't leave, I ran for my life."

"You could have done so with me."

"Could I? And where would I have been if you failed to destroy him, then had enough of me, as I'm sure you would have sooner or later, and discarded me *then*, after I made a mortal enemy of him?"

His glance was haughtiness itself. "There was no pos-

sibility I wouldn't destroy him." His eyes narrowed with…
reproof? "And I promised you protection."

"You dare make it my fault I ended up in mortal danger
when you executed your plan? When I couldn't have known
your promise would amount to anything, when you didn't
tell me anything of your real abilities, let alone purpose?"

"You dare ask why I didn't when you were his accomplice?"

A bitter scoff escaped her. "You promoted me from pas-
sive accessory to active accomplice in under an hour? Wonder what you'd make me by the end of this conversation."

"Whatever *you* call what you did, my desire for you
didn't blind me to the probability you'd run to him if I con-
fided in you. It would have been an opportunity to entrench
yourself further in his favor, adding indebtedness to his already pathological infatuation with you. And I was right."

She closed the mouth that had dropped open at his preposterous interpretations. "Yeah? How so?"

"When a choice was to be made, not knowing my real
'abilities,' you chose the man you thought more powerful.
This indicates what you would have done had you thought I
was a threat to your billion-dollar meal ticket." He shrugged
his massive shoulders. "Not that I blame you. You thought
you made the right choice based on available information.
That you were grossly misinformed and therefore made a
catastrophic mistake doesn't make you a victim."

Protests boiled in her blood. But there was no point in
voicing any. She had no proof, as he'd said.

Even if she did, to whom would she submit it? To him?
The mastermind of her misery?

Her shoulders slumped as the surge of aggression he'd
provoked drained. "You have everything worked out, don't
you?"

"Very much so."

She exhaled in resignation. "So you orchestrated everything, got the result you desired, while even Fate indulged

you and gave you the bonus of a mark to enjoy sexually, huh? That must have made your mission of patiently milking me for all I had more palatable."

His shrug was indifference incarnate. "More or less." His gaze shifted to an expression that seemed to sear her marrow. "With one amendment. It wasn't palatable. It was phenomenal."

"I—it was?"

"Along with a dozen superlative adjectives. Being with you was the only true and absolute pleasure I ever had."

He'd already said he'd wanted her. But the way he'd spelled it out now... His words fell on her like a punch, jogging her brain in her skull.

It had been what had most mutilated her, had left her feeling desecrated. Thinking she'd wanted him with every fiber of her being while he'd only reviled her even as he'd used her in every way. Learning that he'd wanted her had just begun to ameliorate her humiliation. But now his claim that it had been as unprecedented to him... It felt genuine. If it was, then at least their intimacies, which had been so profound to her, among all the lies and exploitation, had been real. She could at least cleanse those intensely intimate memories and have them back.

"And that's why I want you to say it, Isabella."

The hunger in his voice and eyes had her heart ramming against her ribs as if unable to bear their confinement.

"I want you to say you've craved having again what we had all those years ago. That every time you closed your eyes, I was there, in your mind, on your tongue, all over you and inside you, giving you everything only I could ever give you."

Every word he said, soaked in hunger, seething with demand, brought a wave of wet heat surging in her core, her body readying itself for its master doing all the things she'd never stopped yearning for.

She still had to resist. Because of what he'd done to her.

Past and present. Because of what he thought of her. What he was. For every reason that existed, really.

"What if I don't say it?"

Those incredible eyes crinkled, those lips that made her every inch ache with the memory of what they could do to her twisted.

"You want me to force you to take what you're dying to take, so you'd have it, and the moral high ground, too? No, my exquisite siren. If I take you now, it will be because you'll tell me in no uncertain terms that you want me to. That you're *burning* for me to. It's that…or you can go."

And it turned out every reason under the sun to tell him to go to hell was nothing compared to the one reason she had to give him what he wanted.

That he was right.

Giving in, she reached out, wound his tie around her hand and yanked on it with all her strength.

Which didn't say much right now. Her tug was trembling and weak like the rest of her. She was that aroused. He wouldn't have moved if he hadn't wanted to.

But her action was seemingly enough of an appeasement. He let her drag him down so his face was two inches from hers.

His virility-laden, madness-inducing breath flayed her lips, filled her lungs. "Now say it."

Voice as unsteady as her legs, she did. "I want you."

"Say it *all*, Isabella."

That cruel bastard had to extract her very soul, didn't he? Just as he had in the past.

Knowing she'd regret it when her body stopped clamoring, *if* it ever did—but she'd sooner stop her next breath—she gave him the full capitulation he demanded. "I wanted you with every single breath these past eight years."

His satisfaction was so ferocious it seared her as his hand covered the one spastically pulling on his tie, untangling it in such unhurried smoothness. Then, like the serpent he was, he slinked away from her. Heartbeats shook her as she watched him sit on the huge couch facing the pool.

After sprawling back in utmost comfort, he beckoned. "Show me."

Not knowing whom to curse more viciously, him or herself, she walked toward him as if on the end of a hook.

Once her knees bumped his, she lost all coordination and slumped over him under the weight of eight years' worth of craving. Barely slowing her collapse with shaking hands against his unyielding shoulders, her dress rode up thighs that opened to straddle his hips. His eyes burned into hers with gratification up until her lips crashed down on his.

He opened his mouth to her urgency, let her show him how much she needed everything he had as her hands roamed his formidable body, convulsed in his too-short-for-her-liking wealth of hair and her molten core rode the daunting rock of his manhood through their clothes.

"I want you, Richard…I've gone mad wanting you."

At her feverish moan he took over, his lips stopping her uncoordinated efforts to posses them. Sighing raggedly, she luxuriated in his domination, what he'd so maddeningly interrupted before.

His hands roved her, melting clothes off her burning body with the same virtuosity that had always made her breathless. His every move was loaded with the precise ruthlessness of a starving predator unleashed on a prey long kept out of reach.

Breaking the kiss, he drew back, his pupils flaring, blackness engulfing the silvered steel as he spilled her breasts into his palms. His homage was brief but devastating before he swept her around, had her sitting on the couch and kneeled before her. After dragging her panties off in one sweep, he lunged, buried his lips in her flowing readiness. She shrieked at the long-yearned-for feel of his tongue and teeth, her thighs spreading wider to give him fuller access to her intimate flesh, which had always been his.

Hours ago she'd been going about her new life, certain she'd never see him again. Now he was here, pleasuring her as only he had ever done.

Was she dreaming all this?

He nipped her bud, and the slam of pleasure was too jarring to be anything but real. One more sweep or suckle or graze would finish her. And she didn't want release.

She wanted *him*.

"Richard...you..." she gasped. "I need *you*...inside me... *please*..."

Growling, he heaved up, caught her plea in his savage mouth, letting her taste herself on his tongue as he rose, lifting her in his arms. Then the world moved in hurried thuds before it stopped abruptly with her steaming back against cool glass.

The idea that Richard was about to take her against a window overlooking the city almost made her come right then.

Plastering her to the glass with his bulk, he locked her feet around his buttocks, thrilling her with his effortless strength. Then he leaned back, freeing his erection.

The potency that had possessed her during so many long, hard rides had her mouth watering, her core gushing. And that was before the intimidating weight and length of it thudded against her swollen flesh, squeezing another plea from her depths. He only glided his incredible heat and hardness through the molten lips of her core, sending a million arrows of pleasure to her womb, until she writhed.

He didn't penetrate her until she wailed, *"Fill me."*

Only then did he ram inside her.

The savagery and abruptness of his invasion, the unbearable expansion around his too-thick girth, was a shock so acute the world flickered, darkened.

Her senses sparked again to him growling, "Too long... too damned long..." as his teeth sank into her shoulder like a lion tethering his mate for a jarring ride. Then he withdrew.

It felt as if he was dragging her life force out with him. Her arms tightened around his back, her hands clawing it, begging his return. He complied with a harder, deeper plunge, blacking out her senses again with the beyond-limits fullness. After a few thrusts forced her flesh to yield fully to him, he quickened his tempo.

Every withdrawal brought maddening loss, every plunge excruciating ecstasy. Her cries blurred and her muttered name on his lips became a litany, each thrust accentuated by the carnal sounds of their flesh slapping together. The scents of sex and abandon intensified, the glide and burn of his hard flesh inside her stoked her until she felt she'd combust.

She needed…needed… *Please…please*…please…

He'd always known what she needed, when and how hard and fast. He gave it to her now, hammering his hips between her splayed thighs, his erection pounding inside her with the cadence and force to unleash everything inside her, until he breached her womb and shattered the wound-up coil of need.

Her body detonated from where he was buried deepest outward, currents of release crashing through her, squeezing her around him, choking her shrieks.

Roaring her name, he exploded in his own climax, jetting the fuel of his pleasure over hers, filling her to overflowing, sharpening the throes of release until he wrung her of the last spark of sensation her body was capable of.

She felt him pulse the last of his seed into her depths, and a long-forgotten smile of satisfaction curved her lips as her head slumped in contentment over his chest…

A rumble beneath her ear jogged her back to consciousness. "Not enough, Isabella…never enough…"

Feeling boneless, her head spun as he strode away from the window, still buried within her depths. Knowing he'd carry her to his bedroom now, she drifted off again, wanting to rest so she'd be ready for round two…

She jerked out of her sensual stupor as he laid her down.

His scent rose from dark cotton sheets to cloak her in its hot delight, compensating her for his loss as he left her body to rid himself of his clothes. Her clamoring senses needed him back on top of her, inside her. She held out unsteady arms, begged for him again.

This time he didn't let her beg long. He lunged back over her, had her skidding on the sheets with the force of his impact. Spreading her quivering thighs, he pushed her knees up to her chest, hooking his arms behind them, opening her fully. Then, lowering himself over her to thrust his tongue inside her panting mouth, he reentered her in a long, burning plunge.

A shriek tore out of her as he forged inside her swollen flesh, undulating against her, inside her, churning soreness and ecstasy into an excruciating mixture as he took her in even more primal possession than the first time. He translated every liberty he was taking with her body into raw, explicit words that intensified the pleasure of his every move inside her beyond endurance. She climaxed all over him again, then again, eight years of deprivation exploding into torrents of sensation, each fiercer than the previous one.

At her fourth peak, he rammed her harder, faster, till he lodged into the gates of her womb, held himself there, roaring his release. Her body convulsed as she clutched his straining mass to her, her oversensitized flesh milking him for every drop of satisfaction for both of them.

At last, he gave her his full weight, which she'd always begged him for after the storm was over, his heartbeat a slow thunder against her decelerating one, completing his domination.

Always able to judge accurately when his weight would turn from necessity to burden, he rose off her, swept her enervated mass over his rock-solid one, dragging a crisp sheet over their cooling bodies.

She wanted to cling to this moment, to savor the descent with him…but everything slipped away…

* * *

Her mind a silent, empty scape, she tried to open lids that felt glued together. How strange. There'd never been peace after Richard...

Richard!

Her lids tore open, almost literally, and there he was. Illuminated by the dim daylight seeping in from the window of what she now realized was a hangar-size bedroom. He was propped up on one elbow beside her, looking down at her, his gaze one of supreme male triumph as he coated the body he'd savagely pleasured in languid caresses.

She was in his bed. She'd begged him to take her—repeatedly. If she could find her voice, she'd do it again right now.

"I didn't intend to rush your pleasure the first...or subsequent times. I wanted to keep you hovering on the edge of orgasm so long, when I finally gave it to you, I knocked you out on the first try."

"You did knock me out every single time," she croaked.

"No. Knocked out as in nothing could wake you up for hours afterward. I did that the last time only." He pinched and rolled one delightfully sore nipple, glided his hair-roughened leg between hers and pressed his knee to the soaked junction of her legs, dragging a whimper from her depth. "But no harm done. It's time to savor driving you crazy."

Her body clamored for him harder than ever. This addiction hadn't subsided; it had gotten worse.

She caressed his face, his shoulders, his chest, reveling in the longed-for delight of feeling him this way. "Your efforts would be in vain. I'm already crazy for you."

"I know. But I want you desperate."

Before she could protest, his tongue thrust inside her mouth, claiming, conquering. His hands, lips and teeth sought all her secrets, sparked her ever-simmering insanities until he had her writhing, nothing left inside her but the need for him to finish her, annihilate her, leave nothing of her.

Clawing at him, crushing herself against him, she tried to drag him inside her. "Just take me again, Richard."

He held her filling eyes, as if gauging if she was truly at his required level of desperation. Seemingly satisfied, from the grim twist of his lips and the flare of his nostrils, he rose above her, leveling her beneath him.

Locking her arms above her head, his knees spreading her legs wide-open, he was where she needed him most, penetrating her in one forceful thrust.

This time the expansion of her already swollen and sore tissues around his massive erection sharpened into pleasure so fierce, it was almost unbearable. Darkness danced at the periphery of her vision. She gasped, thrashed, voiceless, breathless. His face clenched with something like agony as she clung to him as she would a raft in a tempestuous sea.

She sobbed into his lips. "I wanted this every minute…"

"*Yes*. Every. Single. Minute." His growls filled her lungs even as he refilled her, the head of his shaft sliding against all her internal triggers, setting off a string of discharges that buried her under layers of sensations. It all felt maddeningly familiar, yet totally new.

Then everything compacted into one unendurable moment before detonating outward. She shattered.

Her flesh pulsed around his so forcefully she couldn't breathe for the first dozen excruciating clenches. He rumbled for her to come all over him, to scream her pleasure at the top of her lungs. His encouragement snapped something inside her, flooded air into her. And she screamed. And screamed and screamed as he pumped her to the last twitches of fulfillment.

Then he rose above her, supernatural in beauty, his muscles bulging, his eyes tempestuous. He threw his head back, roared her name as every muscle in his body locked and surrendered to his own explosive orgasm.

Instead of fainting, she remained fully aware this time throughout the stages of the most blissful aftermath she'd ever experienced with him.

Suddenly he spoke. "I wasn't satisfied with how things ended with you in the past. It felt…incomplete. And I must have everything wrapped up to my satisfaction."

For long moments she couldn't breathe, waiting for a qualification to tell her she'd jumped to the worst conclusions of his words.

He only validated her suspicion. "I got you here to close your case. If I may say so, I reached a spectacular conclusion."

Feeling as if he'd dumped her into freezing water, she fought to rise to the surface and from his arms.

Without one more word or glance she dragged the sheet off his body, wrapped herself in it and teetered out of the bedroom, looking for the clothes she hadn't been able to wait for him to tear off her body earlier.

She felt him following her, heading to the open-plan kitchen. Her numbness deepened.

When she was dressed, and as neat as she could get herself after he'd ravaged her, she turned to him.

He raised a mug. "Coffee? Or will you storm out now?"

"You have every right to do this." Her voice was thick and raw as it always had been when he'd made her scream her heart out in repeated ecstasy. It intensified her shame. "I deserve whatever you say or do. After all you've done to me, I disregarded all the injuries you caused me and fell into your arms again."

"And even now, you'd fall there again if I let you. But I'm no longer interested. I'm done."

Gritting her teeth against the pain digging its talons inside her, she said, "Then, I can look forward to never seeing you again for real this time. And no matter what you'd like to tell yourself you can get me to do, *I'm* beyond done."

"Yes, you are. That's the other thing I got you here to do. To tell you that."

She frowned. "What the hell do you mean by that?"

"You're done *here*. You will tell your new partners you've changed your mind about the partnership. You will terminate your lease, pay whatever early termination penalty your contract states, then pack your bags and leave this city, preferably the States. And this time, you will never return."

Four

In her first twenty-four years, Isabella had suffered so many brutal blows, had endured and survived them all, she'd believed nothing would shake her or knock her down again.

Then Richard had happened to her. Every second with him, and because of him, had been a succession of earthquakes and knockouts. After he'd exited her life, it had been a constant struggle not to fall facedown and stay there. But it hadn't been an option to give up. She'd had no choice but to forge on. But she'd thought even if she saw him again, whatever madness he'd induced in her, her own ability to experience towering passions, had been expended.

Then he'd reappeared and just by dangling himself in front of her, he'd made her relinquish all sanity and beg for his destruction.

Now there he stood, barefoot, in only pants, leaning indolently on the counter of his futuristic kitchen, looking like the god of malice that he was. He sipped painfully aromatic coffee in utmost serenity, clearly savoring its taste and her upheaval.

But what else did she think would happen after she'd committed that act of madness? Hadn't she already known she'd regret it? Or had she been that pathetic she'd hoped it wouldn't end horribly? That she'd have the ecstasy she'd hankered for without the agony that she'd learned would come with it? Had she even thought of the consequences as she'd grabbed for the appeasement only he could provide?

But this… What he'd ordered her to do wasn't only horrific, it was…incomprehensible.

The numbness of humiliation and self-abuse splintered under the blow of indignation. "Just who the hell do you think you are? How dare you presume to tell me what to do?"

Almost groaning at how clichéd and cornered she sounded, she watched in dismay as he gave her a glance she was certain had hardened criminals quaking in their shoes.

"Trust me, you don't want to know who I really am."

"Oh, I know enough to extrapolate the absolute worst."

Another tranquil sip. "From your defiant response I actually gather the worst you can imagine is nothing approaching the truth. But your misconception might be the result of my own faux pas. If I gave you the impression that this is a negotiation, I sincerely apologize. I also apologize for previously stating you always have a choice. You never do with me. Of course, there are *always* catastrophic mistakes, still categorized as choices, open to you. In this situation, the wrong choice is to stall. I strongly advise you don't exercise it."

Even now, his delivery of this load of bullying was so sexy and sophisticated his every enunciation reverberated in her reawakened senses like a shock wave.

Loathing her unwilling response, she gave him a baleful glance. "I assure you I won't stall. I will ignore you and your deranged demands altogether."

"In that case *my* only choice is to force you. So you're now down to one catastrophic choice, and it's how hard you decide to make this for yourself."

"Give it your best shot. Hard is my middle name."

As she kicked herself for how lame and how reeking of innuendo that had come out, his lips twitched his enjoyment of her slipup.

Out loud, he only said, "I can assure you, you wouldn't like it if I resorted to extreme measures."

"What extreme measures? Are you threatening to off me?"

His eyes turned to slits opening into thunderclouds. "Don't be daft."

It again seemed to insult him she'd suggest he'd physically harm her. But she wasn't falling yet again into the trap of seeing any measure of light in his darkness.

She twisted the strap of her purse around her hand until her fingers went numb. "I guess you don't off people if you could at all help it. You don't put people out of their misery. You didn't even kill Burton, just consigned him to a worse hell than even I hoped for him."

"Are you *extrapolating* what I did to him?"

"No, I know." His eyebrows rose in astonishment-tinged curiosity, and she hugged herself against a shudder that took her by surprise. "I wasn't a kingpin's trophy wife for four years without cultivating methods and sources to navigate his world and to execute an escape plan when necessary."

Heat entered his gaze again, this time tinged with... admiration? "Indeed. The way you wiped your history was a work of art. We must discuss said methods and sources at length sometime. It could be mutually beneficial to exchange notes on how we execute our deceptions."

She watched his mesmerizing face, wondering how he made anything he said so...appealing to her on her most fundamental levels, logic, self-respect and even survival be damned.

The only explanation was that she was sick. She'd contracted a disease called Richard Graves. And it was either incurable or would have to be cured at the cost of her life.

She huffed in resignation. "Nothing I developed could be of use to you. Next to yours, my abilities are like an ape's IQ to Einstein's. And I use fraud only to survive. It's a fundamental part of your career, of your character. Deceit is a preference to you, a pleasure. But you are right."

He raised an eyebrow. "In my advice not to stall?"

"In supposing I'm extrapolating Burton's fate at your hands. I know where you sent him, what that place is. But what is being done to him there?" She shook her head, the nausea she'd felt since he'd told her he was done intensifying. "Even after all I've seen in my life, my imagination isn't twisted enough to conceive what your warped mind could devise, or what you're capable of."

His gaze fixed on her with a new kind of intensity as he put down his mug, straightened from the counter and prowled closer.

Feeling more exposed now that daylight gave her no place to hide, she forced herself to stand her ground. "If physical threats aren't among your extreme measures, what then? If you think your previous warning of exposing me to Rose and Jeffrey stands, it doesn't. I'm walking out of here and going straight to the practice to tell them everything."

His ridiculing glance told her he didn't believe her capable of doing that. Out loud he only taunted, "I'd still have dozens of ways to make you comply."

"Why are you even asking me to do this?"

"I'm not asking you. I'm telling you."

She rolled her eyes. "Yeah, yeah…I got that already. You're the man who says 'jump' and everyone hops in the air and freezes there until you say down. Quit marveling at your unstoppable powers. It got old after the first dozen times. So give me a straight answer already. It's not as if you care about going easy on me, or about me at all."

"Bloody hell, who am I kidding." Without seeming to move closer, he was all over her. Before she could even gasp, he buried his face in her neck and groaned, "It was I who made a catastrophic mistake, Isabella. I'm not done. I'll never be."

Suffocating under the feel of him, the hard heat and perfection of him, with the mess of reactions he wrenched from her depths, she started struggling. "Let me go. *Now.*"

He only carried her off the ground. She opened her lips to blast him and he closed them with a mind-melting kiss, tasting her as if he couldn't stop.

It was only when she went limp in his arms that he let her lips go, barely setting her back on her feet, pouring one final groan of enjoyment inside her.

"Got that out of your system?" She glared up at him, wishing her hatred could melt his flawless face off his skull.

"I just told you there is no getting you out of my system. So let's not waste more time in posturing and theatrics. Let's get past what I said to you earlier."

"Just like that, huh?"

He squeezed her tighter. "It would be more time efficient. I already admitted to being a pillock and a tosser."

"What?"

His lips spread wider at her croak. It wasn't right. Nature was such a random, unjust system, to endow him with such an array of assets and abundance of charisma. But then, that was what made him such an exemplary fiend.

"That means *massive idiot* and *supreme jerk* in the tongue of my people."

"And you think calling yourself a couple of fancy British insults exonerates you and compensates me? I'm sure in your universe you consider tossing a half-assed apology at someone will wipe away any injury you've dealt them. Not in mine."

His eyes sobered. "I got you here thinking I could get closure and move past you at last. I went through the motions but not only didn't I get said closure, I no longer want it."

Needing to poke out his eyes and wrap her legs around him at once, she pushed at him, bracing against the feel of his silk-sprinkled steel flesh. Just remembering what that chest had done to her as he'd tormented her breasts and pounded his potency inside her…

She gave a strong enough shove that he let her go at last. Because he'd decided to, she was sure.

Regaining her footing, she steadied herself. "So you're not even apologizing. You just realized you've jumped the gun, that you didn't get enough of me and want a few more rounds."

He stroked his hands over his chest, as if tracing the imprint of her hands against it. "I want unlimited rounds. And I never thought it a possibility to have enough of you. I only wanted to be rid of my need for you. I no longer want that. I want to indulge that need, to wallow in it." He reached for her again, slamming her against him, cupping one of the breasts he'd ravaged with pleasure. "And before I made that bloody blunder of following through with my no-longer-viable intention, you wanted nothing more than to binge on me, too."

She pushed his hands away from her quivering flesh. "I'm actually grateful for said bloody blunder. It gave me the closure *I* needed, in the form of a vicious slap that jogged me out of my pathological tendencies where you're concerned."

He grabbed both her hands and dragged them up to his face. "Slap me back as hard as you like. Or better still…" He pulled her hands down, pressed them nails first over his chest. "Take your pound of flesh, Isabella. Claw it out of me."

Trembling with the need to sink her nails and teeth into his chest, not to hurt but to worship him, she fisted her hands against the urge and stepped back. "Thanks, but no thanks."

Circumventing him, the soreness of his possession and the evidence of their intimacies between her legs making her gait awkward, made her curse him and herself all over again.

His voice dipped another octave, penetrating her between the shoulder blades. "I'm rescinding my ultimatum."

That made her turn, that mixture of rage and swooning warring inside her. "You're no longer threatening unimaginable punishments so I'd leave and never return? How kind of you."

He covered the distance she'd put between them, eyes boring into her as if he wanted to hypnotize her. "You only need to end your partnership."

Before she took him up on his offer of slashing her hands open on those razor-sharp cheekbones, or breaking her nails claiming a handful of those steel pectorals, he went on, "Give the Doctors Anderson a personal excuse. If you'd rather not, I will manufacture an airtight one for you and pay the penalty for unilaterally dissolving the partnership. But you don't have to worry about that. I'll arrange a far more prestigious and lucrative partnership for you. Better still, I'll establish your own private practice or even hospital."

Head spinning at the total turnabout he'd made, but more at the sheer nerve of his standing there orchestrating her life for her, the utter insanities he was spouting, she raised her hands. "Stop. Just stop. What the hell is wrong with you? Were you always a madman and I never noticed it?"

"I *am* definitely mad, with wanting you. And you showed me you're as out of your mind for me. So you'll stay and we'll pick up where we left off, without the restrictions of the past. I'll acquire a new residence for you close to me, so you won't waste time commuting. You can have anything else you want or need. You can work with anyone in the world, have access to all the funds and facilities and personnel you wish for. I will accommodate and fulfill your every desire."

He dragged her back to him, hauling her by the buttocks against his hardness, his other hand twisting in her hair, tilting her head back, exposing her neck to the ravaging of his tongue and teeth. His growl spilled into her blood at her pulse point. "Every single one."

Her traitorous body melting inside and out for him, she felt she was drowning again. "Richard...this is insane..."

"We've already established I am, for you." He punctuated every word with a thrust, and her voracious body soaked up the pleasure of every rough grind. "I discovered I have been all these years, but my training, and everything else, held it all in check. I no longer want to hold back. And I won't." He took her mouth in a compulsive kiss that almost made her orgasm there and then. He ended the kiss, transferred his possession to the rest of her face. "If you ever thought Burton indulged you, that was nothing compared to what I'll do for you."

Lurching, feeling as if he'd slapped her, she punched her way out of his arms this time, her voice rising to a strident shout. "I don't want anything from you, just like I never wanted anything from him. So you can take your promises and offers and shove them."

He caressed his body where her blows had landed, licked his lips as if savoring her taste. "I'm telling you everything on offer, for full disclosure's sake. You're free to make use of whatever you choose." He captured her hands again, pressing his lips in her aching palms. "But I am compensating you for the termination of your partnership. That's the one thing that's not negotiable."

She snatched her hands away. "Are you done?"

"I told you I could never be done with you."

"Okay, I've changed my diagnosis. You're not insane, you're delusional. On top of having multiple personality disorder. I'm terminating nothing. And I already told you what you can do with your 'compensations.'"

He tutted, all indulgence now. "I'm not letting you go until we get this settled. So let's get on with it so I can leave you to get on with the rest of your day. You have new partners you have to let down easy after all."

"'This' is already settled. And you're letting me go *now*, Richard."

Turning, she strode the long way back to the door. Though slower, his impossibly long strides kept him a step behind her.

At the door, he pressed himself into her back, plastering her against it, seeking all her triggers. But she was finally angry enough to resist and desperate enough to leave.

"Tell your damn pet door to open sesame, Richard."

Taking a last suckle of her earlobe, sending fireworks all over her nervous system, he sighed. The sound poured right into her brain as he mercifully ended their body meld. But instead of murmuring the door open, he leaned on outstretched arms, bars of virility on both sides of her body, and pressed his hands against it.

So it also had palm-print sensors.

The moment the door opened, she spilled outside as if from a flooding tunnel.

Once she reached the elevator, he called out, "I've laid all my cards on the table. It's your turn."

Looking over her shoulder, she found him standing on his threshold, long legs planted apart, hands in pockets, the embodiment of magnificence and temptation. And knowing it.

She cursed under her breath. "Yeah, my turn. To tell you what I want. I want you to take your cards and go to a hell even you can't imagine, where crazy monsters like you belong."

He threw his head back and laughed.

She'd never heard him laugh before.

Rushing into the elevator to escape the enervating sound, she was still followed by his amusement-soaked question.

"Want me to pick you up from work, or will you finish your vital errand and come back on your own?"

She almost stomped her foot in frustration. The elevator buttons made as much sense as hieroglyphics in her condition.

She smacked every button. "I'll willingly go to hell first."

His dark chuckle drenched her again. "The hell for irresistible sirens is the same one for crazy monsters?"

She glowered at him in fuming silence as the elevator doors finally swished smoothly closed.

The moment she could no longer see him, she slumped against the brushed-steel wall…then shot up straight again.

The damn snake must have cameras in here. She'd dissolved all over him all night, and even just now, she wasn't about to let him see he still messed her up, albeit remotely. She had to hold it together until she was out of his range.

By the time she was in her car, one realization had emerged from the chaos.

She'd never be out of his range. There was no place on earth he couldn't follow her to if he felt like it. And he'd made it clear that he had nothing else on his mind right now.

There was only one way out of this. To change it for him somehow, before he took one step further into her life. And destroyed everything. Irrevocably this time.

How she would do that, she had absolutely no idea.

Richard closed the door, stood staring at it as if he could still see Isabella through it.

He could monitor her for real until she exited the building. But he preferred imagining her in his mind's eye. As she stood there in the elevator, letting go of the act of defiance. As she walked to his private parking area where her car was, every step impeded by the soreness he'd caused her as he'd given her and taken from her unimaginable pleasure. As she drove home in an uproar, furious at him yet reliving their climactic night, her every inch throbbing, needing an encore.

Dropping his forehead against the door he'd sandwiched her against, he could almost feel her every thought and breath mingling with his, melding, tangling, wrestling. Just as her limbs had with his, as her core had yielded to him, and clasped him in a mindless inferno. His body buzzed with exquisite agony as his hardness turned to burning steel.

Pushing away from the door, he discarded his pants as he headed to the pool, his steps picking up speed until he launched himself into the air, arced down to slice into the cool water like a missile.

It was an hour before he'd expended sufficient incendiary energy and centered his thoughts enough to consider the exercise had served its purpose. Pulling himself out of the pool, he sat on its edge, staring through forty-foot-high windows at the sprawling green expanse of Central Park, seeing nothing but Isabella and everything that had happened between them.

So. For the first time in…ever, nothing had gone according to his plan. And he couldn't be more thrilled about it.

Though he'd known she'd been his only kryptonite, he'd believed she wouldn't retain any power over him. Even after he'd realized he still coveted her, he hadn't thought there'd been the slightest danger she'd breach his impenetrable armor.

But every moment with her had been pleasure beyond imagining. Even more indescribable than anything he remembered sharing with her in the past. He now realized his invulnerability had only been the deep freeze he'd plunged into when he'd walked away from her, thinking he'd never have her again. He'd stored everything inside him, starting with his libido, which he'd kept behind barricades of thorns and ice. But mere re-exposure to her had pulverized them as if they were cobwebs, thawed him out as quickly as New York's summer sun melted an ice cube.

He'd tried to fool himself into thinking he could apply brakes to the desire that had overtaken him. But even as he'd told her he was done, the thought of losing her again had made him want to take it back at once. The utter contempt that had dawned on her face had made him willing to do anything to erase it, to restore the contentment his words had wiped away.

And he *had* offered everything. Again. Without trying, she'd snared him again. It was a trap he'd eagerly been caught in. She remained the only person who had his se-

cret access code. The one, in spite of every reason on earth
against it, he gladly relinquished power to.

Satisfaction spread like wildfire, pulling at his lips as he
jumped to his feet and headed for the shower.

Once beneath the pummeling water, he closed his eyes
and relived his nightlong possession of her and her captiva-
tion of him. Next time, this was where he'd end their intimacies, soothing and refreshing her before he let her leave
him. He certainly wouldn't end another climactic night together by doing his best to alienate her.

After his contradictory behavior, she'd run away screaming *monster*. *Crazy monster*, to be exact.

She wouldn't come back on her own. No matter how
much she craved him. As he was now beyond certain she
did.

So he had to pursue her. But he predicted that the harder
he did, the more she'd push him away. He had no problem
with that. It would only make the hunt that much more in-
toxicating.

He *would* have her at his mercy and that of the unstoppable passion they shared. This time, he wouldn't let her
go before he was glutted. If he couldn't be, then he wasn't
letting her go at all.

Exiting the shower, he stood in front of the floor-length
mirror, grimacing his displeasure with his too-short hair.

She'd loved it when it had been longer. He'd woken so
many times still feeling her clinging to it as he'd ridden her,
or combing through it languorously in blissful aftermaths.
It had been why he'd kept it razed, thinking it would abort
the phantom sensations. Not that it had.

Deciding to grow it out, he took extra care with his
grooming, but didn't shave so he wouldn't have a stubble
by the time he saw her again. It had driven her out of her
mind when his whiskers had burned her during sex. But
she'd always complained afterward that he'd sandpapered
her. When he hadn't been able to meet her smooth-shaven

as he had last night, he'd learned how to handle his facial hair to keep the pro of pleasuring her without the con of scraping her sensitive skin raw. By tonight, when he had her again, his current stubble would be the perfect length to give her the stimulation without the abrasion.

After dressing in clothes she'd love, he called Murdock. As always, he answered on the second ring. "Sir."

"I need to get into Dr. Sandoval's home."

"Sir?"

Annoyed that Murdock's response wasn't a straight "Yes, sir," he frowned. "I want to prepare a surprise for her."

After a beat, Murdock said, "You didn't read my report."

Suddenly, Richard was at the end of his tether. He was unable to bear a hint of obstacle or delay when it came to Isabella. "What is it with you and your fixation on that bloody report, Murdock? Did you even hear what I said?"

"Indeed, sir. But if you'd read my report, you would have known it wouldn't be wise to break into Dr. Sandoval's home."

"Why the bloody hell not?"

"Because her family is in there."

Two hours later Richard was driving through Isabella's neighborhood, a sense of déjà vu overwhelming him.

He hadn't even known such a place existed in New York. But there it was—Forest Hills Gardens, what looked like a quaint English village transplanted into the heart of Queens.

A private, tucked-away community within the Forest Hills neighborhood, it was based on the model of garden communities in England. Its streets were open to the public, but street parking was reserved for the residents of the elegant Tudor and Colonial single-family homes that flaunted towers, spires, fancy brickwork and red-tiled clay roofs. Wrought iron streetlights inspired by Old English lanterns lined the block, while the curving street grid was lined with London plane and white ash trees.

It felt as though he was back where he'd grown up.

Shaking off the oppressive memories, he parked in front of Isabella's leased residence, a magnificently renovated Tudor.

Glaring at the massive edifice, he exhaled. If he'd been in any condition to think last night, he would have deduced the reason why she'd leased such a big house when Murdock had imparted that information. It was understatement to say he'd been unpleasantly surprised to find out she lived with her mother, a sister and three children.

That put a serious crimp in his plans of relocating her to be near him. Now instead of invading her home to execute the seduction he'd had in mind, he'd come to get the lay of the land and to lie in wait for her.

Exiting his car, he strode across the wide pavement and ran up the steps to her front porch. He rang the bell then stood back as the long-forgotten sounds of children rose from inside.

The last time he'd heard sounds like that had been the day he'd left his family home.

He'd stood outside as he did now, listening to Robert and Rose playing. They'd sounded so carefree with the ominous shadow of Burton lifted, if only temporarily.

Little had his brother and sister known that Burton had only been absent because he was finalizing the deal that would make Richard the indentured slave of The Organization. They wouldn't have been so playful if they'd known it would be the last time they'd ever see their older brother.

Gritting his teeth, he reeled back the bilious recollections as feet approached, too fast and too light to be those of an adult.

Splendid. One of the little people in her stable was the one who'd volunteered to open the door. An obnoxious miniature human to vex him more than he already was.

All of a sudden the door rattled with what sounded like a little body crashing into it. That twerp had used the door to abort his momentum, no doubt not considering slowing down instead. Maybe waiting for Isabella in a home infested with abominations-in-progress who might aggravate him into devouring them wasn't a good idea.

But the door was already opening. It was too late to change his plan. Or maybe he'd pretend he'd knocked on the wrong door and—

He blinked at the boy who'd opened the door and was looking at him with enormous eyes, his mind going blank.

His heart crashed to one side inside his chest as the whole world seemed to tilt on its axis.

Then his mind, his very existence, seemed to explode.

Bloody hell…that's…that's…

Robert.

The bolt of realization almost felled him.

There was only one explanation for finding a duplicate of his dead younger brother in Isabella's home.

This boy was his.

Five

"Who're you?"

The melodious question sank through him, detonated like a depth mine. Observations came flooding in at such an intolerable rate, they buried him under an avalanche of details.

The texture of the boy's raven locks, the azure sky of his eyes, the slant of his eyebrows, the bow of his lips. His height and size and posture and every inch of his sturdy, energy-packed body...

But it was the boundless inquisitiveness and unwavering determination on his face that hit Richard so forcefully it threatened to expel whatever he had inside him that passed for a soul. That expression was imprinted in his mind. He'd seen it on his brother's face so many times when he'd been that same age. Before exposure to Burton had put out his fire and spontaneity and hope, everything that had made him a child.

Even had it not been for the almost identical resemblance, that jolt in his blood would have filled him with certainty. That Isabella had had his child.

This was his son.

"Mauri...don't open the door!"

"Already opened it, Abuela!" the boy yelled, never taking his eyes off Richard. Then he asked again, "Who're you?"

Before Richard considered if he could speak any longer, a woman in her fifties came rushing into the foyer.

Her hurried steps faltered as soon as her eyes fell on him,

becoming as wide as the boy's, the anxiety in them dissi-
pating, a genial smile lighting up her face.

"Can I help you, sir?"

Something tugged at his sleeve. The boy—Mauri—
pursuing his prior claim to his attention. And insisting on
his all-important question. "Who're you?"

Richard stared down at him, literally having trouble remembering the name he'd invented for himself.

The boy held out his hand in great decorum, taking the
initiative, as if to help him with his obvious difficulty in answering that elementary question. "I'm Mauricio Sandoval."

In the chaos his mind had become, he noted that Isabella
had given the boy her new invented surname. He stared at
the small proffered hand, stunned to find his heart booming with apprehension at the idea of touching him.

So he didn't, but finally answered instead, his voice an
alien rasp to his own ears. "I'm Richard Graves."

The boy nodded, lowering his hand, then only said, "Yes,
but who are you?"

"Mauri!"

At the woman's gentle reprimand, Richard raised his
gaze to her, shaking his head, jogging himself out of the
trance he'd fallen in. "Mauricio is right. Telling you my
name didn't really tell you who I am."

"You talk funny."

"Mauri!"

The boy shrugged at the woman's embarrassment, un-
deterred. "I don't mean funny ha-ha, I mean not like us. I
like it. You sound so…important. Wish I could speak like
that." His gaze grew more penetrating, as if he wanted to
drag answers from him. "Why do you speak like that?"

"Because I'm British."

"You mean from Britain?" At Richard's nod he persisted,
"That's not the same as English, is it?"

The boy knew things most adults didn't. "Not exactly. I
do happen to be English, too, or rather, English first, hav-

ing been born in England. But a lot of people are British—and that means they're citizens of Great Britain—but not English. They could be Scottish, Welsh, or some Irish from Northern Ireland, too. But most of those people hate being called British, rather insisting on calling themselves English or Scottish or Welsh or Irish. I say British because the majority of people from the rest of the world don't know the difference. And most don't care."

"So you say British so they won't ask questions when they don't care about the answers. I ask questions because I like to know stuff."

Richard marveled at the boy's articulate, thorough logic, his insight into what made people tick. He was too well informed and socially developed for his age. Isabella and her family were clearly doing a superlative job raising him.

After digesting the new information, the boy persisted. "You still didn't tell us who you are."

At the woman's groan, Richard felt a smile tug at his lips at the boy's dogged determination. It was clear when he latched on to something, little Mauricio never let go.

That trait was more like him than Robert.

On his next erratic heartbeat his involuntary smile froze. He sensed that there was more to Mauricio's insistence than the drilling curiosity of a young and tenacious mind. Could it be the boy was that sensitive he felt the blood bond between them?

No. Of course not. That was preposterous.

But what was really ridiculous was him standing there like a gigantic oaf, unable to carry his end of an introduction with a curious child and a kindly lady.

Forcing himself out of his near stupor, he cocked his head at the boy, that bolt of recognition striking him all over again. "In my defense, you told me only your name, too."

That perfect little face, so earnest and involved, tilted at him in challenge. "You're visiting us, so you know stuff about us already. We don't know anything about you."

Richard's lips twisted at how absurd the boy's rebuttal made his previous comment. It really hadn't occurred to him to consider that simple fact when he'd made it. His mental faculties had been all but demolished.

While the boy was as sharp and alert as his mother. He got to the point and held his ground. As she always did.

He inhaled a much-needed draft of oxygen. "You're quite right. Knowing your name tells me a lot about you, based on what I already know about your…family, while knowing mine tells you nothing about me. You're also right to insist on knowing who I am. It's the first thing you always need to know about other people, so you can decide what to expect from them. Let me introduce myself better this time."

He held out his hand. The boy didn't give him a chance to brace himself for the contact, eagerly putting his hand in his. And an enervating current zapped through him.

He barely withdrew his hand instead of snatching it away, suppressing the growl that clawed at his throat at the lash of sensations.

"My name is Richard Graves and I'm an old…associate of Dr. Sandoval's."

Mauricio ricocheted a new question. "Are you a doctor?"

"No, I'm not."

"Then, what are you?"

"I'm a security specialist."

"What's that?"

Richard frowned. No one had ever asked him that question. When they probably should have. People assumed they understood what he did when most had no idea. That boy didn't presume. He asked so he'd know exact details, build his knowledge on solid ground. As Robert had.

Realizing his shoulders had slumped under the still-intensifying shock, he straightened. "It's a lot of things, actually, and it's all very important and very much in demand. The world is a dangerous place—and that's why your grandmother was rightfully upset that you opened the door. I'm sure she told you never to do that."

The boy sheepishly looked at the woman who was standing there watching them, her expression arrested. "Yeah, she did. Mamita, too. Sorry, Abuela."

Anxious to drive his point home, make it stick, Richard pressed on. "You must promise never to do that again, to always—*always*—do as your mother and grandmother say. Security is the most important thing in the world. I know, trust me."

The boy only nodded. "I trust you."

The boy's unexpected, earnest response was another blow.

Before he could deal with it, the boy added, "I promise." Then his solemn look was replaced by that burning interest again. "So what do you do?"

"I am the one people come to, to make them safe."

"Are you a bodyguard?"

"I'm the trainer and provider of bodyguards. To banks, companies, individuals, private and public events and transportation, and of course my own business and partners— and many other interests. I also keep people's private lives and businesses safe in other ways, protecting their computers, communications and information against accidental loss or hacking."

With every detail, Mauricio's blue eyes sparkled brighter in the declining sun. "How did you learn to do all that?"

With another groan, the woman intervened again. "Mauri, what did we say about not asking a new question every time someone gives you an answer?" Then she squeezed her dark eyes in mortification. "As if my manners are any better!" She rushed toward him and touched him on the arm. Her smile was exquisite, reminding him so much of Isabella, even though she barely resembled her. "Please come in."

Her gentle invitation agitated him even more. The idea of spending more time with that little boy with the endless questions and enormous eyes that probed his very essence felt as appealing as electrocution. In fact, *that* would have been preferable. He'd suffered it before, and he could say for certain what he was feeling now was worse.

Wishing only to run away, he cleared his throat. "It's all right. I don't want to interrupt your day. I'll connect with Isabella some other time."

The woman's hand tightened on his forearm, aborting his movement away from the threshold. "You wouldn't interrupt anything. I already cooked and updated my website where I do some of my volunteer work. Bella stayed overnight at work, but Saturday is her half day, so she'll be home soon."

So Isabella had explained her night away. But that wasn't the important thing now. The pressing matter was the alien feeling coming over him as he looked into this woman's kind eyes. He could only diagnose it as…helplessness. For the first time in his life he was being exposed to genuine hospitality, and he had no idea how to deal with it.

As if sensing his predicament, she patted his forearm, her eyes and voice gentling. "We'd really love to have you."

Corroborating his grandmother's request, the boy grabbed his other forearm. "Yes, please. You can tell me how you learned everything you do. Your job is as cool as a super-hero!"

The woman looked at her grandson with tender reproof. "Mr. Graves isn't here to entertain you, Mauri."

The boy nodded his acceptance. "I know. He's here to see Mamita." He swerved into negotiation mode seamlessly, fixing Richard with his entreaty. "But you have to do something while we wait for her."

At Richard's hesitation, the boy changed his bargaining tactic on the fly. "If your job is top secret and you can't talk about it, I can show you my drawings."

Richard stared down at the boy. He drew. Like him. Something no one knew about him.

His whole body was going numb with…dread? It was

beyond ludicrous to be feeling this way. But he'd been in shackles, had been tortured within an inch of his sanity, and he'd never felt as trapped and as desperate as he did now with those two transfixing him with gentleness and eagerness.

But there was no escape and he knew it. Those two frail yet overwhelming creatures had him cornered.

Feeling as if he was swallowing red-hot nails, he nodded.

Mauricio's smile blinded him as he whooped his excitement, pulling at Richard. Once he had him over the threshold, he let him go and streaked away, calling over his shoulder, "I'll go get my stuff!"

Watching Mauricio disappear, Richard stepped into Isabella's home as if stepping out from under tons of rubble.

The woman closed the door behind him and guided him inside. "I'm Marta, by the way. Isabella's mother, in case you didn't work that out. I don't know if Bella ever talked about me."

She hadn't. Isabella had never mentioned her family. When he'd tried to investigate them as part of his research into her life, there'd only been basic info until she was thirteen. Anything beyond that age had been blank until she'd married Burton. He now knew she'd later wiped out her years of marriage to him, too. But at the time he hadn't bothered to probe the missing parts, thinking them irrelevant to his mission. But he did remember Marta was her mother's name. She hadn't changed her name, either.

Suddenly something else bothered him. He stopped. Marta stopped, too, her gaze questioning.

"Once your grandson puts that logical mind of his to use, he'll realize you didn't follow your own rule about security. You didn't make sure I know Isabella, or if I do, that we're on the sort of terms that make it safe to let me into your home."

She waved his concern away. "Oh, I'm certain you know her, and well enough. And that it's safe to invite you in."

Warmth spread in his chest at yet another thing he'd never been exposed to. Unquestioning trust. Not even Murdock, Rafael or Isabella had trusted him so completely that quickly.

But such trust was unlikely coming from someone of Marta's age, and one who'd grown up in a country where danger was a part of daily life to so many people.

Was she letting her guard down now that they were in the States and in a secure neighborhood? Or because she judged people by appearances and from his she judged him to be refined and civilized? If she was that trusting with strangers, she could expose them all to untold dangers.

He didn't budge when she urged him onward, needing to make sure she didn't make that mistake again, either. "How did you come by that certainty? Did your daughter ever talk about me?"

"No." She grinned. "And she's going to hear my opinion of that omission later." Her eyes grew serious, but remained the most genial thing he'd ever seen. "But in a long and very eventful life, I've learned to judge people with absolute accuracy. I've yet to be wrong about anyone."

He grimaced. "You think you have an infallible danger radar? That's even worse than having no discretion at all."

She chuckled in response to his groan. "So you first feared I drag in anyone who comes to our door, and now you think I overestimate my judgment?" She tugged at him again, her face alight with merriment. "Don't worry, I'm neither oblivious nor overconfident. I am a happy medium."

He still resisted her, imagining how silly they must look, a slight woman trying to drag a behemoth more than twice her size, with him appearing the one in distress.

"What happy medium? You think I'm harmless."

This made her giggle. "I'd sooner mistake a tiger for a kitten." She sobered, though she continued grinning. "I think you're *extremely* harmful. I know a predator when I see one, and I've never seen anyone I thought as lethal as you. But I'm also sure you don't hunt the innocent or the defenseless. I have a feeling your staple diet is those who prey on them."

His thoughts blipped, stalled. How could this woman who'd just met him read him so accurately?

She wasn't finished. "So yes, I let you in because, beyond the personal details I don't know, I took one look at you and knew who you are. In a disaster, and when everyone else is scared or useless, you're the man I'd depend on to save my family."

He gave up. On trying to predict, or even to brace himself for what the next second would bring in this *Twilight Zone* of a household. He also gave up any preconceptions he'd unconsciously formed about Marta since she'd come rushing after Mauricio. Once he did, he let himself see beyond her apparent simplicity to the world of wisdom, born of untold ordeals, in her gaze. This woman had seen…and survived…too much.

A kindred feeling toward her swept him almost as powerfully as the one he'd felt toward Mauricio, if different in texture.

It seemed his weakness for Isabella extended to those who shared her blood. He might have a genetic predisposition to let anyone with her DNA influence his thoughts and steer his actions.

Marta tugged him again, and this time he let her lead him inside.

As they entered a family room at the center of a home right out of a syrupy family sitcom, she said, "Mauri never opens the door, either. I don't know why he did this time."

He pursed his lips as he sat on a huge floral couch that jarred him with its gaiety, considering the austerity he was used to. "He probably sensed that I'm the one to defend his home against invading alien armies…before he even saw me."

She spluttered, causing his own lips to twitch. He'd already known she wouldn't be offended when he poked fun at her, would relish his caustic humor.

Beaming, the eyes he was learning to read held something he didn't wish to translate. "You can joke about it, but you can actually be right. Mauri is an extremely…sensitive boy. There have been a lot of instances when he realized things he shouldn't or felt things before they happened."

Before he decided what to think, let alone formulate an answer, she clasped hands beneath her chin. "Now let me offer you something to drink. And you'll stay for dinner, yes?"

"Maybe Isabella won't want to have me."

"I want to have you for dinner. Mauri wants that, too. Bella can't say no to either of us. So you're safe."

Admitting that it was easier to decimate a squad of armed-to-the-teeth black ops operatives unarmed than resist this tiny woman, he surrendered. "Tea, please. If you have any."

"Bella has us stocked on every kind of tea on earth. It's the only thing she drinks."

It had been him who'd started her drinking tea, addicted her to it as per her admission. So she hadn't stopped. Just as she hadn't been able to stop her addiction to him.

He inhaled deeply, suppressing the acutely sensory memories that flooded his mind. "Earl Grey. Hot."

Clapping her hands, Marta rushed away. "Coming right up."

As she receded, Richard finally made a conscious comparison between her and her daughter.

She was much shorter and smaller, and her complexion, eyes and hair were darker. There were similarities in their features, but it was clear Isabella had taken after another relative, probably her father or someone from her father's side.

Marta was also different in other ways. Though she'd evidently lived a troubled life, she seemed more carefree, more optimistic than Isabella, even younger in spirit. If he'd ever imagined having an older sister, he would have probably wished for someone exactly like her.

He frowned at the strange idea, shaking it off. And all other distractions fell off with it, releasing his mind, letting it crash in the wreckage-filled abyss of reality.

Isabella had given birth to his son.

She'd been pregnant as she'd run for her life.

When had she found out? Before or after she'd fled?

If before, she would have had to run anyway to hide another betrayal from Burton. Or would she have aborted Mauricio, if he hadn't suspected her, to avoid his wrath?

That was a moot question. She'd had Mauricio, so she'd either discovered her pregnancy just as she'd run or afterward.

But why had she kept him? Had she wanted his child? Or had it all been about Mauricio himself? Had she wanted him?

That she'd had him proved it. Whatever she'd felt when she'd discovered her pregnancy, whatever dangers had been present, her desire to have him had trumped it all.

But she'd been on the run and pregnant, and hadn't considered asking him for help. Even before she'd realized he'd been the cause of her predicament.

So why? If she hadn't hated him then, why hadn't she run from Burton to him? He'd waited for her to, had left all channels open hoping she would. For some reason he couldn't fathom, she hadn't.

But if she had, and had told him about Mauricio, what would he have done? He had no idea.

He still had no idea. What to think, let alone what to do.

And here he was, after an explosive reunion with her that had plunged him right back into the one addiction of his life, sitting in her land of overwhelming domesticity, waiting for her mother to bring him tea and her son his portfolio. Not only had every single plan he'd had coming here been vaporized, every other one in his life had been, too.

What the blistering bloody hell would he do now?

What *could* he do?

Nothing. That was what. Nothing but sit back and observe, and make decisions as he went along. For the first time in a quarter of a century he wasn't steering everything and everyone wherever he wished. All his calculations had gone to hell the moment he'd laid eyes on her again. He expected them to remain there for the foreseeable future.

Making peace with that conclusion, he looked around the place. Murdock had said it had been turnkey, so he couldn't use it to judge anything about her or who she'd become.

Or maybe he could. She had chosen the finished product after all. It indicated this was what she wanted for herself, for her family now. The total opposite of what she'd had when she'd been with Burton, a fifty-bedroom mansion with two ballrooms and an attached garage for thirty cars. The demotion to a six-bedroom house with street parking was quite drastic. At most, he estimated this place to rent for six thousand a month, and to sell for a couple of million. While this neighborhood, though elegant, could as well be a row of hovels next to the outrageous hundred-acre estate of her former residence.

So was this what she wanted? An undistinguished upper-middle-class life? A safe, comfortable neighborhood for her family with good public schools for her child? Had she really changed her life so completely around? It appeared so.

And it appeared it had all been for Mauricio.

Mauricio. A son he hadn't known he had for seven years.

He couldn't get an actual grip on that. The shock of discovering Mauricio's existence would only deepen with time.

Almost as shocking had been Mauricio's and his grandmother's behavior with him. He couldn't rationalize, let alone cope with their instant acceptance. No one had ever reacted to him that way. He scared people on sight. At least awed them. He made the most hardened thugs wary, even before they knew who he really was and what he was capable of. So how had they taken to him so immediately?

Then it all happened at once. The sound of china rattling on a tray heralded Marta's approach. Stampeding feet down the stairs indicated Mauricio's. And the front door was opening.

Isabella.

The others, so focused on him as they rejoined him, missed her arrival until she entered the room. He held her eyes—her glorious, murderous eyes—as Mauricio foisted his precious load in his hands before hurtling himself at her. Her mother greeted her with as much joy. Isabella had eyes only for him.

If looks could kill, he would be a riddled corpse by now.

Mauricio fell over himself to fill her in on their whole meeting, word for word. Marta scolded her lovingly for never bringing Richard up. And though Isabella had brought her deadly displeasure with him under control and gave them a face he'd never seen—one of vivacious delight at being home—they seemed to realize that wasn't what she felt about his presence.

Not about to risk her spoiling their dinner plans, as Richard had intimated she might, Marta preempted her by announcing they'd have dinner at once and have tea later.

He had to give it to Isabella. All through what turned out to be an exceptional dinner, crafted to perfection by Marta, she somehow held back from doing what he could feel her seething to do: hurl a fork into his eye.

Along with discovering what superb home-cooked Colombian food tasted like, he found out the answer to a question he'd fumed over just last night. How a dinner could last four hours.

This one lasted even longer. And not because Isabella's younger sister, Amelia, and her two children arrived mid-dinner and extended the proceedings. That was the usual leisurely rhythm in this household. Something he was amazed to find he couldn't only tolerate, but enjoy. The experience was totally alien, but he still navigated it as if he had dinner with a household of women and children every night.

And like Mauricio and Marta, the newcomers immediately treated him as if they'd known him forever. Minutes after their arrival, he learned that Amelia's husband was finishing a contract in Argentina and would join them in the States next year. Until then, they were staying with big sister Isabella. As they had almost since the children were born.

Having grown up in a subdued household with a military father and a conservative mother, he had no idea how loud and lively a family could be. But it did seem everyone was more gregarious than usual on his account. Probably because an adult male presence was a rarity in their lives. The only other male in the family was Isabella's younger brother who lived abroad. But no matter how many men they'd been exposed to, they'd never seen anything like him. Everyone was so intrigued and awed by him and thrilled to have him.

Everyone but Isabella, of course. But she ignored him with such ingenuity, no one but him realized she hadn't given him one word or look all through dinner, even avoiding answering his direct questions without appearing to snub him.

He ate as much as all of them put together, to Marta's delight, who said she'd finally found someone with an appetite to do her efforts justice. When he said it was only expected, since he could probably house them all in his body, she laughed and was only happy her culinary artwork wouldn't have to be reduced, again, to the status of shunned leftovers.

After dinner they retired to the family room and he was served his promised Earl Grey. Mauricio solemnly told him he'd have to postpone showing him his drawings. He didn't trust the younger children to respect his works of art, and they wouldn't have the peace needed to discuss them anyway.

The evening progressed for another hour with everyone asking him a thousand questions, hanging on every word of his answers, laughing readily at his every witticism.

He sat there feeling like a sprawling lion after a satisfying meal, with a pride of lionesses lounging around him and cubs crawling all over him.

Then Mauricio and the younger children, Diego and Benita, started yawning. Marta and Amelia took them to bed, leaving Richard alone with Isabella for the first time.

Without turning her head toward him, just her baleful gaze, she seethed, "You'll get up now, and you'll get the hell out of here. And you will *never* come back."

Sighing in satisfaction that she'd finally talked to him, even to slash him before evicting him, he only sat forward to pour himself another cup of tea.

He settled back even more comfortably, slanting her a challenging glance. "Are you going to make me?"

"I'll do whatever it takes." Her usually velvety voice was a serrated blade. "I got my family out of a country full of thugs like you, and I am never letting one near them again."

Now, *that* piqued his interest. But direct questioning now wouldn't get her to elaborate. He had to get what he wanted indirectly, by giving her more chances to flog him.

"Thugs like me? What kind do you think I am?"

"I can *extrapolate* well enough."

"Shoot."

"If only I could. Right between your snake eyes."

This took him by such surprise he threw his head back and laughed. "If only you knew."

As if his merriment was the last straw, she turned to him, her body rigid with rage. "What's that supposed to mean?"

"Just that I was once code-named Cobra. So your assessment of my reptilian attributes is quite accurate."

"Of course I'm accurate. As for what kind of snake you are, I think you must have been Burton's rival gangster or you'd been sent by another cartel to destroy the competition.

Though your legitimate image was and remains flawless, I know what you really are. A criminal." At his ridiculing pout, she narrowed her eyes. "Don't bother spouting I'm a criminal, too. Take that to the law or shut up. But I'm telling you here and now, I'll go to any lengths to make certain you never come near my family again."

He sipped his tea, luxuriating in how fury intensified her allure. "You knew all that when you not only let me come near you, but let me be all over you and inside you."

"When it was between us, that was one thing. Now you've involved my family, all rules have changed. You don't want to find out what I'm capable of doing to protect them."

"But I do want to find out. Recount some of the unspeakable things you did in their defense. Who knows, maybe I can be deterred after all."

"Anything I previously did is irrelevant. What I'd do would be tailored to you. I'll keep that a surprise."

"Like you did with Mauricio?"

"Why would my adopted son be a surprise to you?"

That was the story she was going with?

From her immediate retort, she'd prepared that story in case he investigated her. He was sure she'd get her story straight with her mother and sister. She thought he wouldn't be able to find the truth in the void she'd created in her past. She had every reason to believe she'd get away with it since Mauricio looked nothing like him. But he wouldn't contest her claim, not now.

Maybe not ever.

She rose, flaying him with her antagonism. "Why did you come here in the first place?"

He drained his cup, put it on the tray and then rose to his feet. She took a step back, and he knew. She didn't fear him coming closer, but her own reaction to his nearness.

All he wanted was to take her against the nearest wall.

Since that was out of the question in her family-infested

home, he shrugged. "I came to find you, and they snared me. Your mother and son are inescapable. As you should know."

"Yeah, right, the unstoppable Richard Graves finally met his immovable objects."

"Very much so. Your mother and son are intractable. Your sister and her little urchins, too. What should I have done in your opinion to deter their determined attentions? Bared my fangs and snapped at them?"

"Gee, I'm sure they'll be thrilled with your opinion of them. But, yeah, one look at your real face and a swipe of your forked tongue and they would have run screaming. But you sat there purring all night like a lion ingratiating himself to a naïve, male-starved pride."

This time he guffawed. Their unlikely situation had made her think of that parable, too. "What can I say? Your mother's cooking can soothe even me, and your little tribe is quite…entertaining. They're such an exemplary audience. And they're yours, so it wasn't in my best interests to scar them for life with the sight of my hood spread out."

"News flash, playing nice with my family wouldn't ingratiate you to *me*, since that's the one thing I won't forgive you for." Before he could answer, her lips thinned. "Enough of this. Give me your word you won't come again."

His eyebrows rose. "You think my word is worth anything?"

"Yes."

Heat surged in his chest. She seemed to believe that, when she shouldn't believe he had any code of honor.

Not willing to corroborate her belief, he said, "Then, maybe you don't know anything about me after all."

Before she could blast him again, he brushed against her as her mother and sister walked in. He promised he'd be back in answer to their new invitation, then took his leave. The women saw him to the door and stood there until he drove away.

Isabella remained in the background. He was sure she was killing him a dozen horrific ways in her mind.

The stimulation of her murderous intentions only lasted a few blocks before reality all came crashing over him again.

He should heed her warning, should walk away. He'd seen her, he'd had her, and after he made sure she stayed away from Rose, he should disappear from her life again.

It shouldn't matter he felt he'd suffocate if he didn't have more of her. It shouldn't matter she'd had his son. A boy who provoked a thousand unknown stirrings inside him. For what would he do with those aberrant feelings?

She hadn't told him she'd had his son, seemed bound on never letting him know. Even without knowing what he *really* was, she knew she mustn't let him near a boy that age.

And she was absolutely right.

For the past seven years he hadn't known Mauricio existed, and Mauricio hadn't known he did.

He would keep it that way.

Six

After Richard left, her mother and sister pounced on her with questions. Isabella expended every drop of ingenuity she possessed into dodging them and validating none of their suspicions.

Those ranged from his being a suitor she wouldn't let close for reasons they couldn't imagine—since as did every woman on earth, they thought him a god and/or a godsend—to the truth. Her mother was the one whose eyes contained the suspicion...the *hope*, that he was Mauri's biological father.

She held it together until she was in her room, prepared for bed, then collapsed on it in a mass of tremors.

So much had happened so fast in that exhilarating, nauseating and terrifying roller coaster since he'd exploded into her life last night. Now his incursion had reached inside her home and within inches of the secret she'd thought safe forever. And it scared her out of her wits.

And that was before she considered that confounding evening he'd spent with them. Every second he'd spent charming her family like the snake he'd admitted he'd been labeled as, she'd felt a breath away from screaming with aggravation and swooning with dread. At the torture's end, she might have stood her ground, and Richard might have walked away, but she didn't think it would end that simply. He hadn't given his word he'd leave her family alone in his pursuit of her. And nothing involving Richard was without long-term repercussions. She was now terrified what his next blow would be and how he'd deal it.

At least she seemed to have steered him away from any suspicion he might have had about Mauri. His age alone must have been a red flag, and she'd gone light-headed holding her breath, expecting the worst. After all the suspense, he'd only made a passing comment and had taken her claim that Mauri was adopted without batting a lid.

But…maybe this very reaction indicated she was overreacting. Maybe even telling him the truth about Mauri would be the best way to end his infiltration of her life.

A man like him, who lived separate from humanity, without connections, who only cared about having the world at his feet, would probably be appalled at the news he'd fathered a son. His lack of curiosity, or the one that had been satisfied by a mere word, indicated that her assessment was probably correct.

Furthermore, this inexplicable visit itself might turn out to be a blessing in disguise. Maybe seeing her in her domestic milieu as a mother, especially to his biological son, would be a too-banal dose of reality, spoiling the fantasy of the wild affair he'd been planning to have with the mysterious femme fatale he seemed to think her. Maybe it would all douse his passion and make him walk away now, not later.

That sounded plausible. There was no way he would involve himself with her now that he'd seen her "tribe." Spending time with her family had probably been a quaint novelty to him, a field experiment in how the other half lived to add to his arsenal of analyzing human beings, to better devise strategies to control and milk them for all they were worth. But there was no way he'd want to repeat it.

He'd only said he would to punish her because she'd dared challenge him. But once he was satisfied he'd made her sweat it out long enough, he'd let her know he never intended an encore.

Once she came to this conclusion, exhaustion, emotional

and physical, descended on her like a giant mallet. She had no idea when sleep claimed her.

She woke up feeling as if she'd been in a maelstrom.

And she had been. Her dreams had been a vortex filled with Richard and their tempestuous time together, past and present. He'd always wreaked havoc inside her, awake or asleep. There'd never been any escaping him. Not in her psyche. She'd just have to settle for escaping him in reality.

By the time she headed to her office, her new conviction that he'd fade from her life again made her wonder if she should come clean to Rose and Jeffrey about her past.

She'd tried to after she'd left Richard yesterday, to deprive him of that coercion card. But their schedules hadn't allowed her to even broach the subject. So she'd scheduled a meeting with Rose first thing in the morning, the one sure way to get a hold of her.

But if Richard disappeared again, should she expose the ugly truth of her history to Rose and Jeffrey? Just the knowledge would scar their psyches. And what if they worried her past would catch up with her and they'd be standing too close when it did? *She* was certain there was absolutely no danger of that, or she wouldn't have taken their partnership offer. But what if they couldn't feel safe with her around?

She stood by her conviction they'd never judge her, would be more supportive than they already were. But if they worried about their family's safety at all, she'd have to leave.

And she didn't want to leave. Them, the practice, her new place. It was the first time she felt she had real friends, a workplace where she belonged and a home.

By the time she opened her office door she'd made her decision.

She'd wait to see what Richard did. If he disappeared again, that would be that. If he didn't...

No. She wouldn't consider that possibility until it came to pass.

Suddenly she found herself plucked from the ground and suspended against the door she'd just closed with two-hundred-plus pounds of premium maleness plastered against her.

"You're late."

A squeeze of her buttocks accompanied his reprimand before he crashed his lips over hers, invading her with the taste of him, the distillation of dominance and danger.

But he was invading more than her essence. He was breaching her last privacy, leaving her no place to hide. Just when she'd convinced herself he'd leave her alone, set her free.

She'd do anything to make him let her go. Even beg.

But his large hands were spreading her thighs around his hips, raising her to thrust his erection up at her core as he dragged her down on it. His tongue filled her again and again, drank her moans as they formed. Reality softened, awareness expanded to encompass his every breath and heartbeat. Nothing remained but Richard and her and their fusion.

"Richard..."

"Yes, let me hear your distress for me, make up for the agonizing night I spent, needing you under me, all around me."

Something shrill cut through the fog of sensations as he undid her blouse and bra, bent to engulf one nipple in his mouth. The first hot suckle almost made her faint with pleasure. Then the clamor rose again until she realized what it was—her mind screaming, reminding her of the threat he posed to her existence and everyone in it.

It finally imbued her with enough sanity and strength to push out of the craved prison of his arms and passion, to stumble away and put her clothes back in order.

"What are you doing here?"

At his question she turned to him with an incredulous huff. "I won't even dignify that by echoing it."

Lids heavy, his gaze swept her in ruthless hunger, strumming her simmering insanity. "I told you to end your partnership with the Andersons. And what did you do? You reported to work yesterday and again first thing this morning. When I made it clear this is the one thing I won't budge on."

She tossed him a contemptuous glance. "You don't have to budge. Only to bugger off, as you say in your homeland."

His lips twisted in that palpitation-inducing smile that seemed to come easier to him since yesterday. "Don't think that because I want you now more than ever I will bargain with you over this. It's not a matter of either you do it or you don't."

"You're right. It's not a matter of 'either or' but 'neither nor.'" At his arching eyebrow, she huffed. "You do know your grammar, don't you? The language *was* coined where you hail from. I will neither end anything with the Andersons nor start anything with you."

A theatric exhalation. "Pity. After everything that happened between us, I would have rather not forced you into complying. Oh, well."

He produced his phone from his pocket, pressed one virtual button. The line opened in two seconds and she heard a deep voice on the other end. She thought it said, "Sir."

Without taking his eyes off her, Richard got to the point of his call at once. "Murdock, I need a court order to shut down the Anderson Surgery Center in forty-eight hours."

With that he ended the call and continued looking at her.

So that was his extreme measure. If she wouldn't leave, he'd take everything from under her. And she had no doubt he could and would do it. And that would only be for starters. In case this somehow didn't work, he would only escalate his methods of destruction.

And none of it made any sense.

She cried out her confusion. "*Why* do you want me to stop working here? What is it to you? Is this even about me or…" A suspicion exploded in her mind. "Is this about

Rose? Did you discover her relationship to Burton and come here to clean up every trace of him, including anybody who knew him? If so, did you only want me out of the way so I wouldn't warn them about you? And now you've decided to strike directly since I didn't cooperate and spoiled your preferred stealth methods?"

As the conviction sank in her mind, from one breath to the next her desperation turned to aggression in defense of her friends. "Burton was a monster who deserved far worse than whatever you've done to him. But she was his victim. Besides that, Rose and Jeffrey are the absolute best people I've ever known, and I'd die before I let you near them. And that's *not* a figure of speech."

As if he hadn't heard her tirade, he cocked his head at her. "How did you come to know that couple?"

"Wh-what?"

"There was no evidence of when you met, or of your developing relationship, not even emails or phone calls, and I want to know how you did this."

"I—I met Rose in a conference in Texas four years ago."

"And? I want to know what led to their asking you to be their partner and not any of their long-term colleagues."

His icy focus shook her. Where was this interrogation heading? "I felt a…kinship to her at once. I guess she felt the same, since she told me her life story as we waited for a late lecturer. I was shocked to realize that Burton used to be her stepfather."

His eyes and jaw hardened. He gestured for her to continue.

"I didn't tell her about me, but that kindred feeling only grew when I knew both of our lives were blighted by that monster. Incredibly, she felt the same way. Afterward and for years, we talked for hours daily, using online video chat. We practically designed and decorated this place that way. She and Jeffrey kept pushing me to come live in the States and be their partner. The moment I could, I took my family and came back, thinking I was giving us all a new and safe life. Then *you* appeared to mess everything up."

His eyes grew heavier with so much she couldn't fathom. "I don't want to mess things up. Not anymore."

"Yeah, right. That's why you're going to shut down the practice Rose and Jeffrey worked for years to build and invested all their money in."

"It's all up to you. Walk out of here, and I do, too."

"You mean you'd leave them alone, for real? You wouldn't have done that eventually anyway?"

"I already said going after them was to force you to leave. I have no interest in sabotaging their business."

"So this isn't about Rose? You're not after her?"

"It is about her." Before his reply sent her alarm soaring again, he reached for her, dragged her against his rock-hard body. "But the one I'm after is you, as you well know. So I suppose we can negotiate after all. Taking everything into consideration, I'll make you a deal."

She squirmed against him. "What deal?"

"I want you out of here. And I want you, full stop. You want me, too, but need to be assured of your family's safety. So here's my deal. You will make use of everything I can give you, will be with me every possible minute that our schedules permit. And I promise to stay away from your family."

His hypnotic voice seeped through her bones with delicious compulsion, until she wondered why she'd ever put up a fight when being with him had always been all she'd ever wanted. And if he promised her family would be safe…

Then he added, "But only if you stay away from mine."

She pushed away to stare up at him, her mind shying away from an enormous realization.

Then he spelled it out. "Burton was my stepfather, too."

Richard had never intended to reveal that fact to Isabella. But he never did anything he intended where she was concerned. Nothing that was even logical or sane. He touched her, looked into her eyes, and his ability to reason was incinerated.

Not that he cared. As he'd told her, so many things had changed in the past forty-eight hours. His previous intentions weren't applicable anymore. He wanted her, had already decided to leave her family situation untouched. Laying down the card of his relationship to Rose now felt appropriate.

He'd always wondered if she'd ever worked out that his revenge on Burton had had a personal element, until last night when she'd made it clear she'd always thought it purely professional. He'd expected the truth to come as a surprise, but the avalanche of shock and horror that swept her at his revelation was another thing he'd failed to project.

Before he could think of his next move, the door opened after only a cursory knock.

And he found himself face-to-face with Rose.

His heart gave his ribs a massive thump as observations came like bullets from a machine gun. Rose's silky ponytail thudding over her shoulder with her sudden halt, the white coat swinging over a chic green silk blouse and navy blue skirt, her open face with its elegant features tensing and the eyes full of affection as she entered Isabella's office emptying to fill with surprise.

He'd checked her schedule, made sure she'd be occupied with patients during his visit. This confrontation hadn't been a possibility.

But it was a reality now.

And finding the sister he'd watched from afar for more than twenty-five years less than ten feet away was a harsher blow than he'd ever thought it could be.

Tearing his gaze away, he turned to Isabella, who was gaping at him as if she hadn't even noticed Rose's entry.

"I'll leave you to your visitor, Dr. Sandoval. We'll continue our business later."

He turned around and Rose blinked, moved as if coming out of a trance. "Don't go on my account."

He gave her his best impersonal glance. "I was just about to leave anyway."

Before either woman reacted, he'd almost cleared the door when Rose caught him by his sleeve.

Dismay soaring, he raised an eyebrow with all the cold impatience he could muster. He needed this confrontation to be over.

"Rex?"

Everything inside braked so hard he realized for the first time how people dropped unconscious from shock.

The sister who'd last seen him when she was six years old had recognized him on sight.

But it was still just a suspicion. Only he could solidify it. Or Isabella, now that he'd revealed his connection to Rose. But knowing her, she wouldn't be the one to do so. So it was up to him.

Feeling his insides clench in a rusty-toothed vise, he made his choice. "You must have mistaken me for someone else. The name is Richard. Richard Graves."

He flicked Isabella a warning glance, just in case. Not that he'd needed to. Isabella seemed to have lost the ability to speak or even blink. But when she regained the ability to talk, if she did tell Rose...

He couldn't worry about that now. He had to get the sodding hell out of there.

Not giving Rose a chance to say anything else, he turned and strode away, fighting the urge to break out into a run.

Once in his car, he drove away as if from an earth fissure that threatened to engulf everything in its path.

Which was a very accurate description.

Everything since he'd seen Isabella again *had* been like an earthquake that had cracked the ground his whole life was built on. He'd thought he could stem the spread of the chasms and return to a semblance of stability again.

But there was no fooling himself anymore. He'd set an unstoppable sequence of events in motion. And if he didn't stop the chain reaction, it would unravel his whole existence.

And everyone else's, too.

Two hours later in his penthouse, after a couple of drinks and a hundred laps in the pool, he had a plan in place.

He'd just gotten out of the shower when the intercom that never rang did.

The concierge apologized profusely, claiming that it was probably a false alarm, since he'd never allowed anyone up in the past six years, but a lady insisted he would want her up.

Isabella. She'd preempted him.

A wave of excitement and anticipation swept him as he informed the concierge that Isabella was always to be let up without question. He ran to dress, but she arrived at his door so fast he had to rush there barefoot in just his pants.

The moment he saw her on his doorstep, he wanted to haul her to bed, lose himself inside her and forget about all they had to resolve and all he had to do.

"Isabella…"

She pushed past him, strode inside. It took him a couple of minutes of following her through his penthouse to realize—to believe—what she was doing.

She was heading to his bedroom. And she was stripping.

Almost every surprise he'd ever had had involved her. This one almost had him launching himself at her as she passed one of the couches, tackling her facedown and thrusting inside her before they even landed on it.

He held back only because he wanted to let her take this where she wanted, to savor the torment of watching her disrobe for him, exposing her glory to his aching, covetous gaze. The contrast between the pitiless seduction of her action and her straitlaced stride made it all the more mind-meltingly arousing.

Once in his lower-floor bedroom, he could barely see
her until he remembered he could turn on the lights with
a whisper.

The expansive space filled with the subdued lighting he
preferred, showcasing her beauty in golden highlights and
arcane shadows. At the foot of his bed, she turned, wearing
only white bikini panties and same-color, three-inch-heeled
sandals. Her eyes were burning sapphires.

He approached, waiting for her to say or do something.
She only stood there looking up at him.

Suddenly the urge to inspect her body, with the insight
of new realizations, knowing she'd given birth to his child,
overtook him. His eyes swept her voluptuousness, luxuriating in her as a whole before basking in each asset separately.

Her hips were lush with femininity, her waist a sharp
concavity, her legs long and smooth, her shoulders square
and strong. Every curve and line and swell of her was the
epitome of womanliness, the exact pattern that activated his
libido. Each inch of her had ripened to its utmost potential.
He now realized it wasn't only time but motherhood that
had effected the change.

Turning his savoring from visual to tactile, he caressed
her buttocks, her back, leaving her firm belly for last. His
skull tightened over his brain as he imagined her ripening
every day with the child they'd made together during one
of their pleasure-drenched deliriums. The idea of his seed
taking root inside her, growing into a new life, that vibrant,
brilliant boy who'd rocked the foundations of his world last
night, turned his arousal into agony. He needed to claim her,
to mark her with his essence again…*now*.

Wrestling with the savagery of his need, he skimmed his
hands up to her breasts. Blood roared in his ears, his loins,
as their warmth and resilience overflowed in his hands. He
stared at the ripened perfection of her, the need to know if
she'd breastfed Mauricio scalding him, the images searing
him body and mind.

Unbidden, another image flared in his mind, heightening the imaginary inferno. Her, holding another baby, one he'd get to see her breastfeed.

Recoiling from the agonizing visions, he squeezed her supple flesh, his fingers unsteady with emotion and mounting hunger as he circled the buds he'd tasted during so many rides to ecstasy, thicker, darker now, and much more mouthwatering. And now he knew why.

Before he bent to silence the clamoring and engulf her nipples, she slithered from his hold and lowered to her knees.

Mashing her face into his loins, she kissed his erection, her hands trembling over the zipper, dragging his pants down.

"I didn't get to touch and taste you again…"

Her gasp of greed as he thudded heavily in her waiting grasp juddered through him. Relief and distress speared through him in equal measure as she worshipped him, the only touch and need he'd ever craved, measuring his girth, rubbing her face over his length, inhaling and smooching and nibbling. Then with a stifled cry of urgency, she opened her mouth over his crown, swirled her hot tongue over its smoothness, moaning continuously as she lapped up the copious flow of his arousal as if its taste was the sustenance she'd been starving for.

The sight alone, of her kneeling in front of him, of her gleaming head at his loins, of her lips, deep rose and swollen and wrapped around his erection, almost made him come.

Stepping out of what felt like burning cloth, he tried to savor it all, caressed the hair that rained over her face, held it away in one hand so he could revel in her every move and expression, bending to run his other hand over the sweep of her back, the flare of her hips. But she started rubbing herself sinuously against his legs like a feline in heat and he lost the fight.

He dragged her up, growling. Before he threw her back

on the bed and mounted her, she climbed him, wrapped her legs around his hips and ground her moist heat over his erection. He tore her panties off, digging his fingers into her buttocks, making her cry out, crash her lips into his.

Her tongue delved inside his mouth, tangling in abandon with his as if she was bent on extracting everything inside him. He let her storm him, show him the ferocity of her craving, rumbles of pained pleasure escaping from his depths.

Her voice, roughened by abandon, filled him. "Take me, Richard. Or should I call you Rex?"

He could swear he heard a crack as loud as a sonic boom. It was his control snapping.

He thrust up into her, invading her molten tightness, sheathing himself inside her to the hilt in one fierce stroke. Her scream felt as if it tore out of his own lungs. The very sound of unbearable pleasure, as his bellow had been.

On the second thrust he roared again and staggered with her to the bed, flinging their entwined bodies on it, loving her squeal as the impact emptied her lungs, then again as his weight crushed her next breath out of her.

He rose between the legs clamped over his back, holding her feverish eyes, tethering her head with a hand twisted in her hair, the other nailing her down by the shoulder.

Her swollen lips trembled over her anguished demand. "Do it, do it all to me."

He obeyed, pounding her, each ram wrenching from their bodies all the searing sensations they could experience or withstand.

Her shrieks of ecstasy rose until she mashed herself into him and he felt her shatter around him. Her inner flesh gushed hot pleasure over him, her muscles wrenching at his length in a fit of release. He rode the breakers of her orgasm in a fury of rhythm, feeding her frenzy.

"Come with me…"

He did, burying himself to her womb and surrendering to the most violent orgasm he'd ever known even with her, filling her with his essence in jet after excruciating jet.

Following the cataclysm, he couldn't separate from her. Couldn't imagine he ever would. He had to have her like this always, fused to his flesh through the descent, feeling her aftershocks and fulfillment.

He didn't think anything of her receding warmth until she shivered. Frowning, he rose off her to reach for the covers, groaning at the pain of separating from her body.

Securing her under them with him wrapped around her for extra warmth, he smiled in possession and satisfaction down at her. "I take it you've decided to take my deal?"

"No. This was actually the closure we both needed before I told you that I won't."

His hands, which had been caressing her back and buttocks, stilled. Her eyes were unwaveringly serious. She wasn't teasing or resisting. She meant this.

Then she told him why. "I can't have you in my life and hope it would remain normal. I've struggled too long and too hard, have too many people who depend on me to introduce your disruptive, destructive element in my life. I'm the pillar of my family and if you damage me, and I'm sure you will, everything will come crashing down. I won't have that."

Rising to look at her, he felt he'd turned to stone inside and out as she watched her rising, too.

"For closure to be complete, so we'd never have any loose ends tangling us in each other's lives, I'm also here to have everything out once and for all. It's the only way we could both finally let each other go. For good this time."

Seven

Richard let Isabella leave his side, a jagged rock in his throat. This felt real. And final.

Anything he did now to stop her would have to be true coercion. And no matter that he was losing his mind needing her, and she'd proved again she needed him as much, overpowering considerations had made her decide to quell that need. He *could* force her. But he couldn't. He had to have her not only willing, but unable to live without having him.

He watched her careful progress to the bathroom in only her sandals, what had remained on all through. She soon exited and, without looking at him, bent to pick up her panties, dropping them again when she realized they were ruined before walking out. Pulling on his pants, he followed her as she retraced and reversed her stripping journey.

Once beside the pool, she sat on the couch where they'd almost made love the first night and looked at him.

And the *way* she did…as if he was everything she wanted but could never have.

Before he charged her and overrode her every misgiving, her subdued voice stopped him in his tracks.

"I'll start." She stopped to swallow, her averseness to coming clean clearly almost overwhelming. "I'll tell you everything. My side of the story. But only if you promise you'll reciprocate and tell me the whole truth, too."

"What if I promise, and you tell me everything I want to know, but I don't deliver on my end of the bargain?"

Her shoulders jerked dejectedly. "I'd do nothing. I can do nothing anyway. The first truth I have to admit is that I am at your mercy. The imbalance of power between us is incalculable. I have so many vulnerabilities while you have none. You can force me to do anything you want."

He made her feel this way? Defeated? Desperate? He'd thought she needed his chase before she gave in to what she'd wanted all along. But if she truly hated it, this was as insupportable, as abhorrent, to him as when she'd thought he could harm her.

Feeling his guts twisting over dull blades, he came down to sit beside her. "You previously said you considered my word worth having. If you really think so, you have it. A caveat, though. You'll probably end up wishing you hadn't asked for the whole truth. It will horrify you."

"After what I've been through in my life, nothing ever would again." Her gaze wavered. "Can I have a drink first?"

Her unfamiliar faltering intensified his distress. He'd never seen her...defenseless before. Besides the shame that choked him for being what made her feel this way, a piercingly poignant feeling, akin to the tenderness only Rose had previously provoked, swamped him. For the first time he wasn't looking at Isabella as the woman who made him incoherent with desire, a woman he wanted to possess, in every meaning of the word, but a woman he wanted to... protect. Even from himself.

Especially from himself.

Stunned by the new perception, he headed to the bar and mixed her one of the cocktails she liked.

For a year after he'd left her, whenever he'd made himself a drink, he'd made her one, too, as if waiting for her to materialize and take it.

The day he'd thrown Burton in the deepest dungeon on the planet, he'd looked at the cocktail glass he'd prepared with such care and faced the stark truth that she never would. And he'd smashed it against the wall. Then he'd furiously and irrevocably terminated every method of communication she hadn't used. He'd been convinced she'd forgotten him. And he'd hated her then, with a viciousness he hadn't even felt for Burton. Because he hadn't been able to forget her.

And all that time she'd been running, pregnant with his child, giving birth to him, facing endless difficulties and dangers he could only guess at.

He didn't have to guess anymore. She'd finally tell him.

He poured himself a shot of whiskey, breaking his rule of not exceeding two drinks per day. He had a feeling he'd need as much numbness as he could get for the coming revelations.

It seemed she felt the same way as she gulped down the cocktail as soon as he handed it to her. Even with little alcohol, for a nondrinker like her, having it in one go would affect her as much as half a bottle of hard liquor would affect him.

As soon as he sat, struggling not to drag her onto his lap, she said, "To explain how I became Burton's wife, I have to start my story years earlier."

His every muscle bunching in dreadful anticipation, he tossed back his drink.

"You probably know my early history—that I was born in Colombia to a doctor father and a nurse mother and was the oldest of five siblings. My trail stops when I was thirteen, when my family was forced out of our home along with tens of thousands of others.

"Though we ended up living in one of the shantytowns around Bogota, my parents gave me medical training, while I home-schooled my siblings. Everybody sought our medical services, especially guerillas who always needed us to patch up their injured. Then one day, when I was nineteen, we went to tend to the son of our region's most influential drug lord, and Burton, who was there concluding a deal, saw me. He later told me I hit him here—" she thumped her fist over her heart "—like nothing ever had."

His own heart gave a clap of thunder he was surprised she didn't hear.

He wasn't ready to listen to this. Not just yet.

Rising, he strode to the bar to grab a tray of booze this time. He had a feeling he needed to get plastered. He only hoped he could achieve that.

He poured them both drinks. She took hers, sipped it, grimaced when she realized it was a stiff one, but took another swallow before she went on.

"He came to our domicile later to 'negotiate' with my parents for me. My father refused the 'bargain' point-blank and was so enraged he shoved Burton. Next moment, he was dead."

Richard stared at her, everything screeching to a halt inside him. Burton. He'd killed her father. Too.

She adjusted his deduction. "Burton's bodyguard shot him for daring to shove his master. Before I could process what had happened, Burton put a bullet through the killer's head then turned to me, apologizing profusely. My mother was frantically trying to revive my father, while I faced the monster who'd come to buy me.

"The sick infatuation in his eyes told me resistance would come at an even bigger price to the rest of my family. Though my soul wretched at being at this monster's mercy, I'd already dealt with the worst life had to offer and knew I could do anything to survive, and to ensure the survival of my family. And if I manipulated his infatuation, someone of his power could be used to save my family, and many, many others.

"So I swallowed my shock and anguish, said I believed he hadn't meant any of us harm, but to give me time to deal with my shock and loss and to get to know him. He was delighted my reaction wasn't the rejection he'd expected after the 'catastrophic mistake' of my father's murder and he promised me all the time in the world. And everything else I could want. I told him I only wanted my family to be taken to the United States, to live legally in safety and comfort. He told me that would only be the first of thousands of things he'd lavish on me.

"The next day I stood at my father's grave with the man who'd been responsible for his murder. Before Burton took us away, I promised my friends I'd be back to help as soon as I could."

His hand shaking with a murderous rage he'd never before suffered, he reached for the bottle. He took a full swig and savored planning the new horrors he'd inflict on Burton.

Isabella continued, "Within a year he got us permanent residences through an investment program. My sisters and brother were in school and my mother volunteered in orphanages and shelters. Burton pulled strings to equate my experience to college courses necessary for medical school. Then on my twentieth birthday, he proposed. Though he was like putty in my hands, from his murderous behavior with others, I didn't doubt he could kill us all if I wavered now that he'd fulfilled his end of the bargain. I was forced to accept. With an ecstatic smile."

This. The missing pieces. What explained everything. Rewrote history. Made everything he'd thought or felt or done not only redundant or wrong, but a crime. Against her.

And she wasn't finished telling him how heinous that crime had been. "After the lavish wedding, I played the part of the doting wife, capitalized on his abnormal attachment to me. Thankfully, I didn't have to suffer through many sexual encounters, as he rarely wanted full intimacy. I perfected the act of loving his constant pawing, though."

The rage that exploded inside him threatened to crack his head open as he imagined her succumbing to Burton's touch while her every fiber retched at the violation...

He hurled the half-finished bottle across the pool. His fling across dozens of feet was so forceful, the window smashed on impact, exploding outward. If not for the terrace, it would have rained shards on the street below.

Isabella's heavenly eyes turned black at his violence.

He gestured that he'd expended it, would rein it in now, and for her to continue.

So she did. "I was also thankful he'd had a vasectomy in his early thirties. When he said we could still have a child if I wished, I assured him my younger siblings always felt like my children, and I wanted to focus on my education, my humanitarian work, but mostly him. He was delighted, as he was with everything from me. I continued to perform the role of perfect wife to such a powerful man, appearing to make flamboyant use, as he wished me to, of his wealth, and managed to put aside millions. I wanted enough personal power, education-, money- and knowledge-wise, to plot my family's escape from this nightmare. Then you appeared in my life."

Before he found words to express the torrents of regret accumulating inside him, she looked away, eyes glittering.

"When you asked me to leave with you, promised to protect me, I believed you had no idea what you were getting yourself into, not knowing the extent of my vulnerability, or of Burton's power and obsession with me. I thought even if you'd managed to spirit my whole family away, he'd find us, and you wouldn't be able to protect yourself, let alone us, from his vengeance. Oblivious to your real powers, I thought you were no match for him, was certain I'd only doom all of us if I left with you.

"Then you were gone as I always knew you would be one day and I discovered what true misery was at last. It wasn't being trapped in this horror with my family eternal hostages, their lives depending on my ability to perfect my act forever. It was to know what passion was, then to lose it and return to my cage to pine for you forever."

"Isabella…"

Her hand rose, stopping his butchered groan. It seemed

she needed to spit this out, as she would venom. "When you put your plan in action, I knew once he became convinced I betrayed him, he would be as insanely vicious as he'd been irrationally indulgent, so I took my family and ran. Then around a year later, my 'lady in waiting' who was married to his new right-hand told me Burton's bank accounts had been emptied by unknown parties and he no longer had means to buy allegiance or even protection, and that just before she'd called me, he'd disappeared. She suspected he'd been killed.

"Not willing to gamble on that, I decided to go back to Colombia when friends enlisted my urgent assistance in relocating them. I employed all necessary secrecy methods, and used the money I'd taken from Burton to build shelters and medical centers for those I couldn't help personally.

"After three years of no developments, I dared to go back to the States for a conference, where I met Rose. Then four years later, when she kept persisting with her partnership offer, I made my most extensive investigations yet. It was then I discovered you'd thrown Burton into that off-the-grid dungeon for the world's most dangerous criminals and finally felt secure enough to come back. A week later...you appeared again. And here we are."

Richard stared at Isabella, every word of her revelations a shard shredding his guts.

He'd lived among corruption and perversion so long, he considered only the worst explanation for anyone's actions. He'd condemned her at face value, hadn't reconsidered when all his being had kept telling him otherwise.

But what she'd been through wasn't unique. He'd seen worse crimes perpetrated against innumerable individuals in the world he inhabited. It was what she'd achieved in spite of all the danger and degradation, the way she'd conquered all adversity, built unquestionable success and helped countless others that elevated her from the status of coping victim to that of hero.

And he was the villain. One of the major causes of her ordeals. Even worse, among her unimaginable sufferings, he'd been the one to cause her the most anguish.

And she had yet to mention what must have caused her the most turmoil.

"What about Mauricio?"

She turned, her eyes eclipsed by terrible memories. But there was no attempt to hide anything in them anymore.

"He's your son."

He'd already been certain. Still, hearing her say it was a bullet of shame and regret through the heart.

"I discovered my pregnancy just before Burton suspected I might have exposed his secrets. I would have had to run anyway even if he never did, since he would have considered I betrayed him in a way that mattered even more to him. I gave birth to Mauri four months afterward, almost three months before I was due. For weeks I thought I'd end up losing him or he'd suffer some major defects. It took the better part of a year before I was finally assured there were no ill effects of his being born so premature."

Their gazes locked over the knowledge of yet another crime on his record. Her emotional and physical distress as she'd escaped a madman's pursuit while carrying the burden of her whole family, not to mention her grief over losing him, must have caused her premature delivery. And what she'd suffered during and after… His mind almost shut down imagining the enormity of her torment.

"But as I said before, I hadn't put two and two together at the time. So I named him Ricardo, after you."

The consecutive blows had already numbed him. This new one gashed him the deepest. But he'd lost the ability to react to the agony, just welcomed suffering it.

"By the time I worked out what you'd done, and I couldn't bear being reminded of you every time I called him, he was two. It took him a year to get used to being called by his second name, my father's, and another to forget his first one."

So she'd cherished remembering him for two years every time she'd called their son, until she'd discovered his exploitation and the treasured memories had turned to bitterness and betrayal.

His eyes lowered, seeing nothing but a scape of roiling darkness where the most extreme forms of self-punishment swirled in his imagination like hideous phantasms.

"Now it's your turn."

Raising his gaze to hers, he no longer even considered not giving her the truth. Not only what she'd asked for, but *his* whole truth. Every single shred of it.

What no one else knew about him.

Isabella felt as if she'd just turned herself inside out.

But besides nearly collapsing after she'd poured everything inside her out to Richard, she felt…relieved. More. Freed. She'd never shared this with anyone. Even her mother and siblings. She'd protected them from the burden of the full truth. Though her mother suspected a lot, she'd never caused her the injury of validating her suspicions or inflicting the details on her.

Now only Richard knew everything about her.

His only overt reactions had been to bring half the bar over, guzzle down half a bottle, then smash a window fifty feet away. Apart from that, it was as if he'd turned to stone. He'd had no response to finding out Mauri was his.

He raised his gaze to her, his eyes incandescent silver, his face an impassive mask. And she knew he'd keep his word, would tell her his side of the truth. He'd warned it would horrify her. She'd claimed nothing ever could again.

But she'd lied. Her defenses were nonexistent where he was concerned. Anything with or from Richard devastated her. He was the only one who could destroy her.

Then he started.

"My father was in the Special Forces in the British army before he was dishonorably discharged. Bitter and suffering from severe financial problems after many failed investments, he joined a crime syndicate when I was six. He'd trained me in all lethal disciplines since I can remember, and I was so good that he involved me in his work. Not that I realized what we were doing for a couple of years. Then one day five years later, when Rose turned one, his partners came to tell us he'd been killed. Shortly thereafter, one of those partners started coming to our home. Then one day soon after that, my mother told me she and he just got married and the man—Burton—would now live with us."

Isabella sat forward, poured herself a drink, having no idea what it was. He'd already knocked her over with the disclosure that Rose was family and Burton had been his stepfather, too. She had a feeling she'd need anything to bolster her for the rest of his revelations.

"I knew Burton had killed my father because he wanted my mother. He'd been fixated on her as he had been with you. But because my mother was nowhere in your caliber, he soon began to mistreat her. And I could do nothing about it.

"Like you, I had a home filled with vulnerable targets, and though already a formidable fighter, I wasn't fully grown. Even if I could have killed him, that would have destroyed my family. I would have been put in a juvenile prison and my mother wouldn't have been able to carry on without me. So I did as you did. I played the part of the obedient boy who looked up to him, kept him placated every way I could. I tried to curb my younger brother, too, but Robert couldn't understand why I was being so nice to him. Rose soon took Robert's side, and it became Burton's favorite pastime to abuse them verbally, mentally and then, finally, physically. I hid my murderous hatred, channeled the perfect disciple, knowing it was the only thing that kept him in check, that he could easily kill them as he had our father."

She gulped down the horrible liquid in her glass, her eyes

filling. His gaze showed no indication of his thoughts as he continued recounting his atrocious past like a nuance-less automaton.

"When I was around sixteen, Burton started displaying signs of big money. I sucked up to him even more to find out its source, until he said he was now working for a major cartel just called The Organization, who turned abducted or sold children into mercenaries. He said he could make a bundle if he gave them Robert and Rose, that it would serve the two brats right.

"Knowing he'd do just that, I said surely their price would be a one-time thing, but if I became one of their 'handlers,' they'd pay me big money continuously, and he could have it all. Burton didn't like that it seemed I was protecting my siblings when I always said I could barely tolerate them. He also thought it fishy that I'd offer to give him the money I worked for. I allayed his suspicions, say-ing I considered it a benefit on all sides. I'd get out of the dump we called home, get rid of my clinging family, and get the best on-the-job experience. The money was in re-turn for giving me this opportunity, as I wouldn't be doing anything with it for years, with all my needs paid for by my new employers."

Isabella had heard of The Organization many times dur-ing her marriage to Burton. The magnitude of evil they perpetrated was mind-numbing. To learn that Richard had volunteered to basically be sold to them to save his siblings, to save Rose, was…too much to contemplate, to bear.

"Buying my rationalization, and knowing how much The Organization would pay for my skill level, Burton jumped on my offer. I knew I'd leave my family behind, but the al-ternative was incomparably worse. The last time I saw them was the day I left to join The Organization. Robert was ten and Rose was six.

"I intended to amass enough power to one day assassi-nate Burton untraceably and disappear with my family. But he kept guarding against any counterstrikes. I know I never let my loathing show, but Burton, being the self-preserving parasite that he was, moved my family to places unknown, kept obliquely threatening me with their safety, providing me with evidence they were all well. As long as the monthly flow of cash continued."

She had the overwhelming urge to throw herself at him and hug the helplessness he must have felt out of him. But Richard wasn't one for human compassion, giving or receiving it. And if he ever were, she wouldn't be the one he'd seek that from.

Oblivious to her condition, he went on, clearly bent on giving her the whole story in one go, as she had been.

"What made that first year in The Organization survivable was a boy two years younger than myself. They called him Phantom, considered him their star future operative. Then Burton noticed the friendship we thought we'd hidden. He monitored us and overheard Phantom saying he was working on an escape plan. Burton told me if I reported him it would mean a higher place in The Organization at once and more pay. *He* couldn't do it, because he'd have to say how he'd found out, and I'd be punished for not reporting my *friend's* plans, would be demoted, or worse, when Burton wanted my paycheck to move to the six digits already. He had a lot of investments going. He made it clear it was Phantom…or my family."

Isabella struggled to hold back the tears. She'd always thought Richard made of steel, that he'd never felt love or fear for others, let alone could be held hostage by those feelings. And for him to have been just that, by the same man who'd caged her in the same way, was too much to contemplate.

"I knew Phantom, being prized, would be punished, tortured, but not killed. My family were nowhere as valuable. And there were three of them. Burton could hurt or even kill one to have me toe the line the rest of my life. So I re-

ported Phantom. I let him think I did it to advance my standing within The Organization so he'd hate me and show it,
to further reinforce my coldblooded image, which everything depended on.

"Then I went all out to prove myself to be the absolute
best they ever had. I applied my ruthlessness in ways you
couldn't begin to imagine, my body count rivaling all the
other operatives put together, until my monthly income was
in the eight figures, with most of it going to Burton. I'd
hoped to inundate him with far more money than he'd ever
dreamed of so he'd let my family go, or at least treat them
better until I got them out.

"But my escape and retaliation plans were further com-
plicated when I was put in charge of another child—a boy
they called Numbers, who reminded me so much of Robert. I couldn't leave him or Phantom behind. But I finally
gained enough autonomy so I could search for my family.
I found them in Scotland…only too late. I pieced together
that my mother tried to escape with my siblings. Burton
pursued her and she lost control of her car and drove off
the side of a mountain."

Isabella lost the fight, let the tears flow.

Richard didn't seem to notice as he continued reciting
Burton's unimaginable crimes against him and the ghastly
sequence of events of his loss.

"From what I learned, Burton hadn't bothered to help or
to report the accident. He'd just walked away, since they'd
already served their purpose. My mother and brother had
died on impact. Only Rose had survived. I found her in an
orphanage and arranged for her adoption by a kind and
financially secure couple who'd been about to immigrate
to the United States. I've been keeping an eye on her ever
since."

And that, Isabella realized, was how he'd found her again.
Even though the paranoid way she'd conducted her relationship with Rose had kept her under his radar that long.

His dark voice interrupted her musings. "I never considered telling Rose I was alive. Then today... I can't believe she remembered me." He looked downward, his scowl deepening as if he was reliving those fraught moments. Without raising his face, he raised his eyes, impaling her with his glance. "What did you tell her after I left?"

She swallowed. "Nothing. I pretended I got an urgent call from my mother and ran out."

He only gave a curt nod. "It's best for her to remain ignorant of my existence."

She couldn't contest his verdict. Rose's life was the epitome of stability. The last thing she needed was his disruptive influence destroying her peace.

Although... he'd handled her crawling-with-kids-and-chicks household with stunning dexterity...

No. That had been a one-off. He'd sought her out the very next day to tell her he'd stay away from her family. Richard wouldn't want anyone permanently in his life. Not even his long-lost sister. Certainly not one who came with an extended family life right out of the textbook of normal and adjusted.

Considering he was done with that subject, he resumed his tale. "It was years before I could put my escape plan into action, after I made sure Numbers and Phantom and their team had escaped. I followed them, but as expected, they decided to kill me."

She gasped, blood draining. Phantom had been under the misconception he'd been his heartless enemy, a threat to their freedom and lives. As she'd been until an hour ago.

"Did you finally tell him the truth?"

He shrugged. "I saw no point."

"No point?" she exclaimed.

"Yes. I'd done everything they knew me to be guilty of, everything they hated me for. It didn't matter why I did it."

"Of course it matters. Knowing why always matters!"

He shook that majestic head of his in pure dismissal. "I don't believe so. I own my crimes, I don't excuse them."

He wouldn't ever think of asking forgiveness for them, either. "So if you didn't cite your extenuating circumstances to change their minds, how did you do it?"

"I told them it was in their best interest to back down, since it was them who wouldn't survive a confrontation."

A huff of incredulity escaped her. "I bet you weren't even exaggerating."

His look was what she expected a god would give a mortal who asked if he could smite him down. "I never exaggerate. They're formidable warriors, but their genius is in intelligence, applied sciences, medicine and subterfuge. My virtuosity is in termination."

"You're no slouch in intelligence and subterfuge yourself," she mumbled, remembering how he'd totally taken her in. Suddenly a terrible thought crossed her mind. "But since you survived without a scratch, does that mean…?"

An eyebrow arched. "You think I'd spend years planning to help them escape, only to kill them when they got their knickers in a twist?"

She exhaled in relief. "So how did it end with both sides alive, if you didn't put them straight and antagonized them in the most provocative method you could?"

"I was just stating facts. If they hadn't been using their macho hindbrains, they would have realized if I was the enemy, they would have all been already dead. Luckily, before I had to drive my point home, Numbers put himself between us and they backed down only for him. I let them continue thinking what they liked. I wasn't interested in becoming their friend, just in leading them in establishing our joint business."

"All your partners in Black Castle Enterprises are escapees from The Organization."

It wasn't a question but a realization. And it explained

everything. Those men were all larger-than-life; they must have been forged in the same hell Richard had been.

He nodded. "Once I made sure they were safe and our plan to dismantle The Organization was in motion, I could finally take my revenge on Burton. You know the rest."

No. She'd only thought she did.

It turned out she'd known nothing.

Now she did. And the more everything he'd just told her sank in, the more baffled and devastated she was. It *did* horrify her. But not in the way he'd thought.

He'd thought knowing he'd been the top executioner in such an evil establishment would validate her suspicions about him and…well, horrify her. What agonized her was realizing how much more nightmarish his life had been than hers. And that he'd had the best justification for all he'd done.

In fact, believing her to be Burton's willing wife, it was a wonder he hadn't punished her as viciously as he had him. It said a lot about the extent of his desire that it had curbed his killer instincts and stayed his hand.

Not that such desire mattered now. Those earth-shaking disclosures didn't change a thing.

While he might still want her, everything that had happened to him in the past had made him what he was now. If there was one man on earth who was unavailable for anything…human, it was him. That he hadn't said a thing about Mauri was proof positive of that.

So what she'd come here to tell him stood. She couldn't afford to have him in her life.

No matter that she craved him like a drug.

Her priority remained Mauri.

Inhaling a breath that burned like tear gas, she rose to her feet. He remained sitting, not even looking at her.

She waited until he looked up. "It's great we got things out in the open. But now you know my real history, you know I am not a danger to Rose, either myself or by association. Now we can go our separate ways, never to cross paths again."

Before he could say anything, she turned and rushed away.

It turned out she didn't have to worry. He just brooded after her in silence.

Once at the door, she remembered he had to open it for her. Before she could walk back to ask him to, the door opened. She hurried out, relieved, demolished.

This was it. It was over for good this time.

She'd never see Richard again.

Eight

When Rose entered her office the next morning, Isabella wasn't a mute, paralyzed mass like yesterday. She was a hopeless, miserable one.

She still struggled to smile as she received her treasured friend and colleague. Rose returned her kiss on the cheek before she pulled back, her blue-gray eyes filled with suppressed questions. She must be bursting to have her suspicion about Richard validated.

"Everything okay at home?"

In spite of the concern lacing the question, and the text message she'd sent her last night, Isabella believed Rose hadn't bought her excuse for running out yesterday one bit.

But Rose always made it clear that she was there for anything Isabella needed, and left it up to her to reveal any problems or worries. Isabella had never told her anything. Until now.

After she'd held it all in all these years, now that her family and those she'd struggled to help were safe, she could allow herself to consider her own needs. And now that the one she'd shared her innermost turmoil with had exited her life forever, she needed another confidante. Someone who wouldn't only listen in silence, offering not a word of sympathy or support, as Richard had. The only one who fit the bill was Rose.

She sat her down. "I need to tell you something—important. A lot of things, actually. About my past."

The worry hovering in Rose's eyes mushroomed into anxiety. "I always knew you were hiding something big, kept wishing you'd tell me."

Isabella reached for Rose's hands. "Before I do, I want you to promise to act according only to your and your family's best interests."

Rose grimaced. "Shut up and tell me everything, Izzy!"

And she did. Everything minus Richard.

All through her account, Rose's expressive face displayed her shock, horror, anguish and outrage on her behalf in minute detail. Her tears came at one point and wouldn't stop until Isabella fell silent and she hurled herself at her and crushed her in a nonending, breath-depleting hug.

"God, Izzy, you should have told me!" Rose sobbed between hard squeezes. "Why didn't you tell me?"

Isabella's tears flowed, too, as she surrendered to Rose's searing empathy. *This*…this was what she'd needed all these years, what she'd deprived herself of.

She thankfully let Rose inundate her with frantic reprimands before she finally pulled away, her tremulous smile teasing. "That's why I didn't tell you. I was afraid you'd drown me and flood the practice. Like you're doing now. When we've just finished decorating."

Rose burst out laughing. "God, Izzy, how dare you make me laugh after what you just told me?"

"Because it's all in the past. I just needed you to know everything about me, needed to share what I can't share with even my mother. But it is really all behind me."

Rose's resurging tears suddenly froze, her face filling with reproof again. "What did you mean by that prefacing warning? If you thought it a possibility this would change anything between us, you're stark raving mad!"

Isabella's heart expanded at the proof of her friend's magnanimity and benevolence. Then it compressed again. "Don't make any decisions now. Take time to think about it."

"The only thing I'll do with time is fume for months that you didn't come to me with this years ago!"

Isabella's lips spread at her friend's steel conviction. "At least wait until you see what Jeffrey thinks."

Rose's eyes widened. "You want me to tell Jeffrey?"

"I just assumed you would tell him."

Rose looked terminally affronted. "Of *course* I won't tell him!"

Isabella reached a hand out to hers. "I want you to tell him."

Rose snatched her hand, fisted it at her chest. *"No."*

It was Isabella's turn to burst out laughing at the growling finality in Rose's usually gentle, cheerful voice and the furiously obstinate expression that gripped her gorgeous if good-natured face. She looked like a tigress defending her cub. Isabella's laughter made her crankier.

Isabella tried to suppress her smiles. "I consider Jeffrey part of you. Not to mention a part of us, our team."

"I said no. You told *me* because you needed to purge the burden from your system by sharing it with someone who's strong enough to carry it with you, someone you fully trust."

"That's absolutely right, but Jeffrey—"

Rose cut her off. "You also needed to have someone fully appreciate what made you the wonderful human being you are."

"Uh…not that I'm not delighted you think I'm wonderful, but that's not how I…"

Again Rose bulldozed over her protests. "I tell Jeffrey all my secrets not because he's my husband and soul mate, but because they might impact him, so he's entitled to a heads-up. But if you really wanted him to know, and thought he should, as himself, not as a part of me or our team, you would have sat us both down and told us both all that. But you chose to tell only me."

Isabella shook her head at the incredible combination her friend was. The most romantic person on earth who melted

with love for her husband, and the most no-nonsense prag-
matist around. And as she'd always known, the best, stron-
gest, most dependable friend anyone could aspire to have.
She always felt the fates had chosen to compensate her for
all the hardships of her life with Rose. And now she'd unburdened herself to her, not to mention knowing her relationship to Richard and therefore to Mauri, she felt the uncanny
bond they'd shared from the start had become even deeper.

"And you did because I'm your closest friend. We're even
closer than I thought. We both had our souls almost shattered by the same monster. And we both survived him."
Rose's eyes shone with admiration. "Though I can't begin
to compare our ordeals at his hand. I didn't fight for my
life and that of my family for years like you did. I survived
by accident."

Isabella now knew that wasn't true. Beyond escaping
death in her family's car crash, Rose's survival had been
no accident. She'd been saved. By Richard. He was the one
who'd created her second chance in life. He was the real
difference between their lives. She hadn't had a savior and
champion like him.

She couldn't tell Rose that. The older brother who'd been
looking out for her since she was ten didn't want her to
know.

But although she'd always thought he'd played the opposite role in her life, that of conqueror and almost destroyer,
it was still him who'd rid her of Burton forever. That made
him the one who'd given her this new lease on life.

"What about Mauri? Is he…?" Rose choked. She couldn't
even say Burton's name.

"*No.* I would have never let myself get pregnant by him."

But she *had* let herself get pregnant by Richard. When
she'd discovered her pregnancy, even after he'd left, even
knowing the danger she'd put herself in, she'd been giddy
with delight that she'd have a part of him with her always.

So far, she'd risked it again. Four times, if she wanted to be accurate.

Rose's voice dragged her out of her turbulent musings. "Whew. It's a relief to know that monster didn't manage to perpetuate his genes."

Grabbing the opportunity to steer the conversation in a less-emotional direction, she pulled a face at Rose. "You should know me better than to think I'd inflict those on my child."

Rose pounced, hugging the breath out of her before pulling back. "But you're so amazing your genes would vaporize any dirt or perversion in any others. Mauri would have turned out to be the awesome kid he is just because you're his mom."

Feeling suddenly lighthearted, when she'd thought she'd never feel that way again after losing Richard for the second and last time, Isabella dragged Rose closer and smacked kisses on both her cheeks.

"Have I told you lately just how much I love you?"

Rose gave her a mock scolding glare. "When have you ever told me that?" When Isabella started to protest, Rose pulled her into another hug. "You never needed to tell me. I always knew. And I love you, too. Now more than ever."

Isabella hadn't expected to go home happy. But thanks to Rose, and to work, not to mention to Prince Charming Jeffrey, the day she'd predicted would be an endless pit of gloom had turned out to be the best she'd had in a couple of decades.

She didn't expect her buoyant condition to continue, knew misery would descend on her more aggressively than it had the first time she'd lost Richard. Back then, there'd been distractions vying for her mental and emotional energy, fractioning her turmoil over him. Now, without anxieties consuming her focus, she'd experience the full measure of it.

There was another reason she was certain her despondency would only deepen. Before she'd met him again, she'd had this vague hope she'd find love again. She now knew this was an impossible prospect.

Richard would remain the one who could make her turn off the world and lose herself in his ecstasy. She didn't want—couldn't stomach—anything less than that. So now she knew. She'd spend the rest of her life as a mom, a daughter, a sister, a friend and a doctor. But the woman part of her was over. Only Richard had the secret code to this vital component of her being. And he was gone. Forever this time.

Turning onto her street, she shook herself. She was sliding again, and she owed it to Mauri and her family not to expose them to her dejection. She'd promised them a shining new beginning and she'd be damned if she didn't deliver.

And then she had to count her blessings. She'd unburdened herself to Rose, their bond had become more profound, her family was safe, they loved their new home and she loved her new workplace. If she obsessed over Richard more than ever, if her body demanded its mate and master now that she could no longer swat her hunger away with hatred…tough.

She'd just mentally slapped some sense into herself when she saw it.

Richard's car. Parked—again—in her spot.

Her heart followed the usual drill when it came to Richard. It crashed to a halt before bursting out in mad gallop, stumbling like a horse on ice.

She didn't know how or where she ended up parking, or how she made it inside the house. The empty house. Where was everyone…?

Shouts burst from the kitchen. Her heart almost exploded from her chest as she burst into a run, then she heard… clapping. *Clapping?*

Screeching to a halt at the threshold, she saw…saw…

Richard was in her kitchen. He had every member of

her household at the huge semicircular counter island and he was…

Performing for them. Knife tricks.

He was swirling knives with such speed and skill, his hands were a blur; the feats he performed with four—no, five…*six* knives nothing short of impossible. He made it look effortless. His captive audience was openmouthed and glassy eyed.

She sympathized. She would have done the same if she wasn't shocked out of her wits.

With everyone hypnotized by his show, they didn't notice her. Only he slunk her a sideways glance, that half smile that reduced her brain functions to gibberish on his lips. She stopped behind Mauri, and Richard escalated the level of difficulty, catapulting knives above his head, behind his back, turning this way and that to show them the intricate, mesmerizing sequence.

At the crescendo of his routine, he tossed what looked like a fish filet in the air, threw the knives in blinding succession after it, slicing it to equal pieces in midair. After catching the plummeting knives in one hand and the fish pieces in the other, he spread his arms and took a bow.

A storm of applause and yells erupted. She almost clapped and cheered, too. Almost. It was a good thing she was still breathing and on her feet.

Everyone's excitement intensified when they noticed her. Richard slinked a tea towel over his shoulder as he approached her, his gaze unreadable, his mouth curved in that devastating smile. Her head filled with images of her winding herself around him, dragging that arrogant head down and taking those cruelly gorgeous lips.

"Did you catch Richard's unbe*lievable* show?" Amelia exclaimed.

"I caught a slice of it." Everyone laughed at her reference to his closing act. Including him. She wanted to be mad at him for crashing her home again, but couldn't. But that didn't mean she couldn't still reprimand him. "How will I convince the kids not to play with knives now?"

He waved away her concern. "I already took care of it."

"Oh, how did you do that?"

"I told them only I was allowed to do such things, as I spent more years than they've been on this earth practicing."

"And this convinced them?"

"They are extremely obedient cubs."

She blinked. "Uh, are we talking about the same trio?"

"*Or* I'm too intimidating even when I'm trying not to be."

Said trio was flitting around preparing the kitchen table, their awed eyes almost never leaving Richard. "They don't look intimidated, they look enthralled."

"Same result." His smile grew placating. "Don't worry. I got their promise they'd never try anything with sharp objects. I promised Mauricio I'd teach him to juggle. With environmentally safe plastic."

Before she could hiss his skin off for making Mauri such a promise, he turned to his audience.

"Now, to the second part of my show. Food."

Her mouth hung open as her mother and sister rushed to empty three huge brown bags on the other counter.

"Richard brought everything to make sure his recipe is just right," her mother explained, her smile so wide it hurt Isabella. "We're having a cooking contest. You'll grade his efforts tonight against mine in our first dinner face-off."

As Richard started preparing his ingredients, Isabella closed her mouth to keep her jaw from dragging on the floor.

Was that really him? Was this even her home? Or had she stepped into some parallel universe?

He wasn't kidding about this being the second part of the show. He turned preparing seafood into feats of speed and precision. She was sure he assembled weapons and dismantled bombs with the same virtuosity.

All the time he quizzed the kids about the seafood, spices, herbs and vegetables he used. Their excitement at the informative and entertaining Q and A session was almost palpable. She'd never seen them so taken with an adult. Mauri asked him more personal questions than she'd thought possible, down to how he chewed his food. Richard was a good sport, rewarding Mauri's boundless curiosity with amusing, frank, yet age-appropriate answers.

Seeing them interact the first time had been disturbing. Now it plain hurt.

After Richard started cooking, he said, "Somebody recently taught me that recipe. I was the sous chef during its preparation. Now I get to be the chef and, fingers crossed, I won't turn what was a magical seafood feast into a curse."

Amelia, who'd taken her eyes off Richard only to swing them to Isabella for a silent verdict on how things stood between them, piped in at once, "You have nothing to worry about. The aromas alone are a powerful spell."

"Who taught you this recipe?" That was Mauri, of course.

"A lovely lady called Eliana."

If he'd thrown that knife he wielded into her heart it wouldn't have hurt more. Hearing him mention another woman with such indulgence made something she'd never felt on his account sink its talons into her gut.

Jealousy. Acrid, foul. And totally moronic. She was the one who'd turned down his offer to continue their intimacies.

But…he'd never cooked with her!

Well, he was cooking for her whole family now.

As if he could feel her burning envy of that woman who'd taken him into her kitchen and made him follow her orders, his steel-hued gaze targeted her. "She's almost like a sister to me since she married a man I consider a brother."

The tension drained from her muscles, forcing her to sit.

Mauri's next question came at once. "What's his name?"

"Rafael. Ah-ah…" Richard raised his hand, anticipating and answering Mauri's next batch of questions. "Rafael Moreno Salazar. He's from Brazil and he's my partner.

He's ten years younger than me. And *he* is a magician with numbers."

Numbers. The boy Richard wouldn't leave behind in The Organization, the one he'd postponed his own escape for.

Forever needing more info about Richard, Mauri lobbed him another question. "Do you have other friends?"

"I have six partners, including Rafael. One I considered my best friend. He doesn't like me back now."

And that had to be Phantom.

Before Mauri pounced to extract that story, Richard gave him what she could only call a man-to-man look that said, "Later." And wonder of wonders, it worked. Well, almost.

Mauri swerved into another tack. "What's his name? Where's he from?"

"Numair Al Aswad. That means *black panther* in Arabic. He's a sheikh from a desert kingdom called Saraya."

Everyone's eyes got even wider. It was still Mauri who asked what she thought was on everyone's mind. "Is each of your friends from a different country?"

Richard chuckled as he began to distribute food on plates. "Indeed. Black Castle Enterprises is a mini United Nations. We also have a Japanese chap, a Russian, an Italian and a Swede. My right-hand man, Owen Murdock, is an Irishman. I trained him like I trained Rafael."

"Like you'll train me?"

It felt as if everyone, except Benita and Diego, who chose this moment to bicker, held their breath for Richard's answer.

He considered Mauri for a moment. "We'll see if you've got what it takes first."

"I got it!"

The kids giggled at Mauri's impassioned claim but stopped at once. It wasn't Mauri's scolding look that made them look so sheepish and contrite. They never reacted like that to his "older brother" exasperation. It was Richard. He didn't level any disapproval or reprimand at them, just a look.

She fully sympathized. Just a look from him took control of her every voluntary and involuntary response.

Her mother and sister intervened to end Mauri's bombardment of Richard, and they all sat to eat.

It did turn out to be a magical meal, on all counts. The food was fantastic, making everyone want to meet the Eliana who'd invented the recipe, with her mother the first to declare Richard the winner of their contest. The constant mood was one of prevailing gaiety and excitement, again thanks to Richard. He was a maestro in handling people of all ages, compelling, constantly surprising, making each person feel they had his full attention, and causing them to fall over themselves to win his approval.

Although she knew this was just his expert manipulation skills, she couldn't help but enjoy it. Delight in it. But both his behavior and her reaction to it made her more nervous.

What *did* he want?

Then she was finally getting the chance to find out.

After dinner, her mother and sister insisted she and Richard retire to the living room while they cleaned up. Mauri agreed to stay behind only after Richard promised a drawing session afterward.

The moment they were out of earshot, she pounced. "Any explanation for…all of this?"

A smile that should be banned by a maximum-penalty law dawned on his face. It was different from what he'd flooded her family and house with all evening. A mixture of wickedness and provocation. One of those would have been more than enough for her to handle. Together, as with everything about him, they were overkill.

He only answered after he sat. "Your family invited me, remember?"

"And since when do you answer anyone's invitations?"

"You have no idea what I've had to do in the past months with Rafael's marriage. Then Raiden, another of the Black Castle blokes, the Japanese-by-birth guy I mentioned, followed suit. Both their weddings had me putting up with human beings all the time. Then came Numair's. That one rewrote the fundamental rules of existence for me. He was the one I thought would be the last man on earth to succumb to the frailties of our species or fall into the trap of matrimony. Nothing was sacred after that, and I've been open to anything ever since. Even cooking dinner from a minitribe of women and children."

So all his friends had married. Was that what was making him dip his foot in the land of domesticity? To see if it was for him? And he thought her household was the most convenient testing ground, since he already had a son and a lover there? Did he think she'd let him experiment on them?

Gritting her teeth, she sat beside him. "You said you'd leave my family alone."

"That was only in return for leaving mine alone."

"But you now know your concern for Rose is misplaced."

"I do. I no longer want you to stay away from Rose."

"Well, *I* want you to stay away from my family."

"I no longer want to do that, either."

"Why? You only involved my family as a pressure card."

"I did?" He cocked his head at the grinding of her teeth. "By 'family' you mean Mauricio. You want me to leave *him* alone."

"Who else?"

At her exasperated answer, he shrugged. "I don't want to do that, either."

"Why?" she snapped. "What's new? You didn't bat a lid when I told you he was your son."

"I didn't because I've already been immunized against the shock, having contracted it full-force the day before. I knew he was my son the moment I saw him."

"No *way* you knew that. He looks nothing like you."

He produced a picture from his inner pocket, handed it to her. If she wasn't certain Mauri never had clothes like that, and this photo was in a place they'd never been and looked from another era, she would have sworn it was him.

"That's my younger brother, Robert. He looked exactly like our mother. I took after my father. Rose was a mix of the two."

Stunned, she raised her eyes, a memory rushing in. "Rose once told me Mauri so reminded her of one of her dead brothers. I didn't make anything of it, as it never occurred to me to tie you to her."

His face darkened. "So she believed I was dead."

She swallowed. "She did only because it was the only thing to explain why you didn't search for her."

His jaw muscles bunched. She winced at the pain she felt for both Rose and him. This wasn't right. That he'd deprived Rose of knowing he was alive. Rose suffered the loss of her biological family even now. And he might have suffered even more watching her from afar.

"But she didn't hesitate to identify you, which means she's been clinging to the hope that you're alive. You probably look very much like she remembers you."

"I was sixteen. I looked nothing like this." He lowered his gaze, as if remembering those moments they'd all been frozen with shock, each for their own reasons. "Did she ask you about me again?"

"I didn't give her a chance. I told her everything about me, so she was too busy with my revelations to think of you. But I'm sure she will. What do you want me to say when she does?"

"What do you want to tell her?"

That was the last thing she'd expected he'd ask. "I…I honestly don't know. I think she deserves to know the brother she loved and clearly still misses terribly is alive. But you probably have nothing in common with that brother, so maybe it's not in her best interests to know you. It's your call."

"Don't tell her."

Hating that this was his verdict, but conceding it was probably the right one, she nodded.

Then her original point pushed to the forefront again. "So you knew about Mauri all the time you were here before, and as I told you everything about myself. Yet you gave no indication that you were in the least interested."

"I wasn't." Before her heart could contrarily implode with dismay, he added, "I was flabbergasted."

That astounded *her*. "I didn't know anything could even surprise you."

"Finding a seven-year-old replica of my dead brother on my ex-lover's threshold? That's the stuff strokes are made of."

The "ex-lover" part felt like a blow to her heart.

Sure, she'd walked away this time, saying it was over. But was that what he already considered her? What he'd decided she was? When they'd made love…had earth-shattering sex…just yesterday? If he wasn't here to pursue her, then why was he here?

"I walked out of here intending not to come back."

"And that was the right decision. Why are you back?"

"Because the facts have been rewritten. Now instead of wanting to end your friendship with Rose, I want to be your and your family's…ally."

Ally? *Ally?* That was downright…offensive after what had happened the past couple of days. Not to mention in the past.

"I don't need allies."

"You never know when and how you might. Having someone of my influence on your side can be more potent than magic."

She tamped down the need to blast his insensitive hide off his perfect body. "I have no doubt. But I don't need magic. I work for what I have. And I have more than enough to give my son the best life and to secure his future."

"Even if you don't want or need my alliance, you don't

have the right to make that decision for Mauricio. The fact remains, he's my flesh and blood. And my only heir."

After a moment of gaping at him, her nerves jangling at his declaration, she choked out, "Are you here because you decided to tell him that?"

Mauri chose this crucial moment to stampede into the living room. "I got all my drawing stuff!"

Before she could say anything more, Richard turned his attention to Mauri.

Brain melting with exasperation and trepidation, she could only watch as father and son ignored her and got engrossed in each other. She had to wait to get her answer.

A no would mean resuming her life as it was. A yes would turn it upside down. And it was all up to Richard.

As it had always been.

Richard had swung around at Mauricio's explosive entry, infinitely grateful for the distraction.

As heart-wrenching as the sight of him, the very idea of him, still was, right now he'd take anything over answering Isabella's question. Since he didn't have an answer for it.

He had no idea what he was doing here, or what he would or should do next.

In the distraction arena, Mauricio was the best there was. The boy—his *son*—wrenched a guffaw from his depths as he hurled himself at him, dropping his armful of drawing materials in his lap.

Crashing to a kneeling position at his feet, Mauricio anchored both hands on his knees and looked up at him with barely contained eagerness. "Tell me your opinion of my work. And teach me to draw something."

"You can draw?"

That was Isabella. She would have asked if he could turn invisible with the same incredulity.

Richard slid her a glance. "I have many hidden talents."

"I'm sure." She impaled him on one of those glances that

made it an achievement he hadn't dragged her out of that kitchen and buried himself inside her.

Mauricio dragged his focus back, and his angelic face, overflowing with inquisitiveness and determination, sent a different avalanche of emotions raging through him.

His throat closed, his voice thickened. "Why don't you show me your best work?"

Mauricio rummaged through the mess on his lap, then pulled out one sketchbook and thrust it at him. "This."

With hands he could barely keep from trembling, Richard leafed through the pages, his heart squeezing as he perused each effort, remarkable for a boy of his age, testimony to great talent…and turmoil.

Had the latter manifested itself in response to their life-style, as Isabella kept relocating them to keep them safe? He was sure she'd shielded her son and family from the reality of their situation. But he believed Mauricio was sensitive enough he'd felt his mother's disturbance, and felt the dangers she'd paid so much of her life to protect him and their family from.

There was also a searing sense of confusion in the drawings, an overwhelming inquisitiveness and the need to know, what *he'd* experienced firsthand. Was that a manifestation of his growing up fatherless? Was he constantly wondering about the father he'd never known, or even known about? Did a boy of such energy and intelligence miss a stabilizing male influence, no matter how loving and efficient the females in his life were?

He pretended to examine each drawing at length, trying to bring his own chaos under control.

At last he murmured, "Your imagination is quite original and your work is extremely good for your age."

Mauricio whooped. "You really think I'm good?"

Though the boy's unrestrained delight made him wish to give him more praise, he had to give him the qualification of reality. "Being good doesn't mean much without hard work."

"I work hard." Mauricio tugged at Isabella. "Don't I?"

Her eyes moved between them, as if she was seeing both for the first time. "You do, when you love something."

Richard retuned his gaze to Mauricio before he plunged into her eyes. "When you *don't* love something, you must work even harder. When you're lucky to love something, it only makes the work *feel* easier because you enjoy it more. But you must always do anything, whether you enjoy it or not, to the very best of your ability, strive to become better all the time. That's what I call 'got what it takes.'"

Mauricio hung on his every word as if he was memorizing them before he nodded his head vigorously.

Isabella's gaze singed every exposed inch of his skin.

The burning behind Richard's sternum intensified as he turned a blank page. "What do you want me to teach you?"

Mauricio foisted the colors at him. "Anything you think I should learn."

Richard gave him a considering look. "I think you need a lesson in perspective." As soon as the words left his lips, Richard almost scoffed. No one needed that more than him right now.

"What's that?" Mauricio asked, eyes huge.

"I'd rather show you than explain in words. We'll only need a pencil, a sharpener and an eraser."

Richard blinked at the speed with which Mauricio shoved the items in his hand then bounced beside him on the couch, bubbling over with readiness for his first drawing lesson.

Gripping the pencil hard so the tremor that traversed him didn't transfer onto the paper, Richard started to sketch. Mauricio and Isabella hung on his every stroke.

Before long Mauricio blew out a breath in awe. "Wow, you just drew some lines and made it look like a boy!"

Richard added more details. "It's you."

"It does look like me!" Mauricio exclaimed.

Richard sketched some more. "And that girl is Benita."

"But she's not that much tinier than me."

"She's not tiny, she's just far away. Watch." He drew a few slanting, converging lines, layered simple details until he had a corridor with boy in front, girl in back. "See? We have a flat, two-dimensional paper, but with perspective drawing, we add a third dimension, what looks like distance and depth."

Mauricio's eyes shone with the elation of discovery, and something else. Something he'd once seen in Rafael's eyes. Budding hero worship. He felt his lungs shut down.

"I get it!" Mauricio snatched another sketchbook, showed him that he did before raising validation-seeking eyes to him. "Like this, right?"

Richard felt the smile that only Mauricio, and his mother, provoked spread his lips. "Exactly like that. You're a brilliant lad. Not many people get it, and most who do, not that quickly."

Mauricio fidgeted like a puppy wagging his tail in exultation at his praise. "*I* didn't know anyone could draw so quickly and so great! Can you do everything that good?"

"As I told you, whatever I do, I do to the best of my ability. I'm the best in some things, but certainly not in drawing. Plenty can do far better." Mauricio's expression indicated he dismissed his claim, making his lips widen in a grin once again. "There *are* people who make it seem as if they're pouring magic onto the pages. But what they and I can do comes from a kernel of talent, and a ton of practice. The talent you have. Now you have to practice. It will only become better the more you do it."

Isabella's gaze locked with his and the meaning of his motivational words took a steep turn into eroticism. It had been incredible between them from the first, but only kept getting more mind-blowing with "practice." That last time had been their most explosive encounter yet. He couldn't wait to drag her into the inferno of ecstasy again.

Suppressing the need, he continued to give Mauricio examples while the boy emulated him. Isabella watched them, the miasma of emotions emanating from her intensifying.

Mauricio finally exhaled in frustration, unhappy with his efforts. "You make it look so easy. But it isn't."

"You'll get there eventually. What you did is far better than I expected for a first time."

Mauricio eyed his drawing suspiciously. "Really?"

"Really. Draw a lot, draw everything, and you'll be superlative, if you want to be."

"Oh, I want!"

"Then, you will be. Trust me."

"I trust you."

A jolt shook Richard's heart. Hearing Mauricio say that again, with such conviction, made him want to go all out to deserve that faith and adulation.

Should he be feeling this way? Was it wise? Could he stop it or had he put in motion an unstoppable chain reaction?

"I want you to teach me everything you know."

Richard laughed. The boy kept squeezing reactions of him that he didn't know he was capable of. "I doubt you'd want to learn most of the things I do."

"I do!"

He slanted a glance at Isabella. "I don't think your mother would appreciate it, either."

"Because it's dangerous stuff?"

"To say the least." Before Isabella burst with frustration he looked at his watch. "And that's a discussion for another day, young man. We agreed we'd do this until your bedtime. Now you need to go to sleep and I need to get going."

Without trying to bargain for more time, Mauricio stood and gathered his things, looking like a stoic knight's apprentice. He had an acute sense of dignity and honor. Once he gave his word, he kept it. It made Richard…proud?

Before he could examine his feelings, Marta came to take Mauricio to bed. Handing his grandmother his things, he came back to say good-night. After he hugged his mother, he threw himself at Richard, clung around his neck.

"Will you come again?"

Feeling the boy's life-filled body against him, the tremor of entreaty in his voice, was like a fist closing over his heart.

Richard looked over the boy's head at Isabella. Her eyes were twin storms. She was terrified. Of where this might lead. Truth be told, he had no idea where it would. And was just as afraid.

But he had only one answer. "Yes, I will."

Planting a noisy kiss on Richard's cheek, Mauricio slipped free, flashing him a huge grin before skipping off.

The moment she could, Isabella hit him with the burning question she'd postponed for the past hour. "*Do* you intend to tell Mauri the truth?"

There was only one answer to that, too.

"No. Not yet."

Nine

Not yet.

Every time those two words reverberated in Isabella's mind, which was all the time, it made her even more agitated.

Not yet implied he would tell Mauri the truth eventually.

But he'd also implied that even if he did, it wouldn't mean anything would change. Mauri would only know he had a father, and would get the benefit of all his wealth and power.

As if *that* wouldn't change everything.

Before he'd left that night, he'd confessed he hadn't thought this through, didn't know what to expect himself. But the fact remained that Mauri had a right to everything he had as his only heir. While he…he only wanted to know his son. Only time would tell how that would translate into daily life or in the long term. They'd just have to wait and see how things worked out.

She had no other choice but to do just that. Now that he'd expressed the wish to know his son so unequivocally, she'd been unable to deny him his desire.

Ever since that day three weeks ago, she'd succumbed and gone along for the roller-coaster ride of having Richard in her family's everyday life. And he'd been with them every possible minute. After their workdays, from early evenings to past the children's bedtime, he'd been there. And he'd shocked her more with each passing minute.

His unstoppable charm continued on full-blast. But she could no longer believe it to be anything but genuine. Though he dazzled them all, she was now certain it wasn't premeditated. He clearly liked being with her family. He really was interested in all of their concerns and indulgent of all their quirks.

But with Mauri, he was something she'd never seen a man being toward a child, not even her own loving father.

That almost tangible affinity they shared had disturbed her, worried her from that first day. It shook her to her core to see it growing every day, in Richard's eyes, in his vibe. Such absolute focus, such a heart-snatching level of emotion.

What shook her as much was seeing *him* through new eyes. There was far more to him than the lethal seducer who'd taken her heart and body by storm, or the merciless void who'd taken Burton apart, or the ruthless manipulator who'd threatened to tear her life apart when he'd first returned. There were depths and passions in him she doubted even he knew he possessed. And no one seemed more surprised to discover these hidden qualities than Richard himself.

Just today, he'd done something she was certain he'd never contemplated within the range of possibilities.

He'd taken them shopping.

She'd agreed only after he'd promised no splurging. After the fact, she'd kicked herself for not defining *splurging*. To him, it could be keeping it under a million dollars.

As it had turned out, she shouldn't have worried.

Thinking they were shopping—rightfully so—with the genie of the lamp, the kids had asked for things they wouldn't dare ask of their family. She'd bated her breath, hating to have to shoot him down in front of them if he succumbed to their demands. But he'd only given them the most subtle but stern lesson in needless excess and its detriments. After that, they'd let him choose, and he'd picked reasonably priced stuff they'd been delighted with, but would also truly enjoy *and* benefit from.

Mauri was the one who didn't ask for anything, excessive or otherwise. He was overwhelmed each time Richard picked something out for him that he revealed he'd intensely wished for. What he'd never asked her for. Mauri never asked for anything, as if he was aware of her burdens and never wanted to add to them, even when she entreated and cajoled him to ask for anything. It forced her to try to predict his desires. Clearly very inaccurately. It upset and stirred her in equal measure that Richard, after such short if intense acquaintance, was the one to read him so accurately.

After the shopping for the kids was concluded, she told Richard he was forbidden from buying the adults anything. He again said she didn't have a right to dictate terms on the others' behalf. She grudgingly conceded that his relationship with her family should remain independent of theirs.

Especially since *that* was now nonexistent.

Ever since he'd come offering his so-called alliance, there'd been no hint of the voracious predator he'd been. Each day, each *hour* that passed without him bringing up his desire for a continuation of their affair left her partially relieved…but wholly distraught. For she wanted him now, this new him she could admire and respect, far more than she'd ever wanted him before. But it seemed her earlier assumption had been correct. The reality of her being the mother of his son, the domesticity of her life situation, seemed to have doused his passion irreversibly.

Just as she was considering putting herself out of her misery and asking him what his intentions were, she found Rose and her family right in their path.

Rose hadn't asked her about Richard again. To her relief. And astonishment. Isabella surmised she hadn't because she feared Isabella knew nothing about his real identity, and didn't want to cause him trouble since he was hiding it.

Following the same rationalization, Rose probably wouldn't bring up her suspicion again in everyone's presence.

As Jeffrey and their kids, Janie and Robbie—named after Rose's mother and brother, Janet and Robert, as Isabella only now realized—rushed to greet them, Rose stood behind, staring at Richard. Richard, after shaking hands with Jeffrey at Isabella's brief introduction, stared back.

After her mother and sister took the kids and went to the food court, only the four of them remained. Jeffrey's animated conversation petered out when he realized it was a monologue and finally noticed the turmoil in his wife's eyes as she stared at the stranger.

Before he could react, Rose threw herself at Richard, clung to him with all her strength.

Isabella's lungs almost burst. Richard looked as if he'd turned to stone the moment Rose touched him.

Then Rose's incoherent whimpers started to make sense. "Don't tell me you're not Rex…don't you dare."

Richard squeezed his eyes shut, bared his teeth as if straining under an unbearable weight.

Rose suddenly pulled back, features shaking out of control, eyes reddened and pouring tears as she grabbed his arms in trembling hands. "You're my brother. *Say* it."

Richard breathed in sharply, emptied his massive chest on a ragged exhalation and nodded. "I'm your brother."

A sob tore out of Rose's depths and she flung herself at Richard again. Among the cacophony filling her ears, Isabella heard Jeffrey exclaiming a string of hells and damns.

As Rose wept uncontrollably, mashing her face into her brother's chest, this time Richard contained her in his great embrace, stroked her gleaming head soothingly, his hands trembling. Isabella remembered to breathe only when she felt the world dimming.

Richard had decided to stop hiding, to let his sister have him back.

A week ago she'd asked him why he'd never done that.

He'd said so he wouldn't taint Rose's life with his darkness. When she'd said that same fear should apply to her and her family, he'd assured her he'd installed every precaution, would never impact them negatively in any way. When she'd countered he should do the same with Rose and come clean to her and his response had been a silent glance, she'd figured it was only a matter of time before he did.

Suddenly it hit her. This was all his doing. He was the one who'd chosen the mall and decided when to stop shopping and walk around. He must have known Rose and her family were coming, had wanted to set this up to see where it would lead. But it seemed Rose had still surprised him with her unrestrained reaction.

Richard now stepped back from the sister who clutched him as if afraid he'd disappear again if she let him go. What Isabella saw in his eyes almost knocked her off her feet.

Such…*tenderness*.

She'd seen nothing like that in his eyes before. Not even toward Mauri. With him there was indulgence, interest, and when no one noticed, stark, fierce emotions that left her breathless. He'd certainly never looked at her—before his current careful neutrality—with anything approaching this…sheer beauty. She hadn't thought him capable of it.

But she'd never inspired such depth and quality of emotion in him.

His voice was a gruff rasp as his gaze moved from Rose to Jeffrey and back. "We have much to talk about. How about we do it over lunch? Isabella wanted to have sushi today."

Nodding feverishly, looking up at him as if at everything she'd ever wished for had come true, Rose clung to his arm, let him steer her away. Isabella and Jeffrey followed the newly reunited siblings in a trance.

Richard spent the first hour telling the Andersons everything. The next two were consumed with Rose's nonstop questions and his attempts to answer each before she hit him with the next.

He left out strategic areas. Such as how many monsters he'd eliminated. And how he'd gotten the info to bring Burton down, making it sound as if Isabella had cooperated knowingly, as if there'd been nothing beyond this goal between them. Rose must have been too dazed to remember her earlier observation that Mauri looked like their dead brother to come up with the right conclusion. But Isabella felt it was only a matter of time before she did. Or before Richard told her.

Jeffrey finally shook his head. "So you removed every obstacle from our path in our known history! I thought we were plain lucky, but Rose always said she had her own guardian angel, and me by association. Turns out she was right."

Richard huffed. "More like a guardian devil."

Rose's eyes filled again as she squeezed his hands. "You've always been an angel to me, from the first moment I can remember, till that day you went away. But I always felt you watching over me, and that's why I never believed in my heart that you were dead. It's only because you never came forward that I had to tell myself that you were. But I lived feeling I'd one day see you again. That's why I knew you the moment I saw you. Because I've been waiting for you."

"I'm glad you did." Richard's smile was tight with emotion. "And I'm sorry I made you wait that long."

She lunged across the table, knocking things over to plant a tear-smeared kiss on his cheek before subsiding. "Never be sorry. I'll be forever grateful you're alive, that you found me back then and that you're here now. I can't ever ask for more than that."

"Can *I* ask you to forgive me for ever doubting you?" Jeffrey hugged his wife to his side lovingly before returning his gaze to Richard. "Rose always talked about her biological family, but mostly about you. Though she had more years with your mother and brother, she remembered you most of all. She always said you were the best at everything, couldn't believe you *could* die. She painted this Superman image of you, and what do you know? She was right. I have a bona fide double-oh-seven for a brother-in-law."

"I bet Rex would put him to shame…uh…" Rose stopped and smiled goofily at Richard, squeezing his hand again as if to make sure he was really sitting across from her. "I don't know if I can get used to calling you Richard."

His free hand cupped her cheek, and the look in his eyes almost uprooted Isabella's heart all over again.

What she'd give to have him look at her that way.

"You have to in front of others." His gaze suddenly turned deadly serious. "It's beyond vital I'm never associated with Cobra, The Organization's operative. Though I wiped every shred of evidence they had on me, changed radically from the bald-shaven, crooked-nosed, scarred boy and man they knew, and no one suspected me in the past ten years, I can't risk any mistakes that might lead to my exposure. The consequences to everyone I know would be unspeakable."

At his ominous declarations, what shook her most was finding out he'd been mutilated by his years as his father's, Burton's and The Organization's weapon. She'd only known him after he'd fixed the damages—at least the physical ones—but now she realized more than ever how deep they'd run.

At the couple's gaping horror, he exhaled. "This is why I didn't want to burden you with my existence. Maybe it's advisable that I continue watching over you from afar without entering your lives at all."

"No!" Rose's cry was so alarmed, so agonized, it was another blow to Isabella. "I *must* have you in my life. We'll do everything you need us to do." She tugged at her husband, eyes streaming again, imploring. "Won't we, Jeff?"

Jeffrey nodded at once, eager to allay his wife's agitation. "It goes without saying, man. Your secret is our secret." Then he grimaced. "But what are we going to tell the kids?"

"Oh, God…I hadn't thought of that," Rose sobbed, the realization bringing on another wave of weeping. "We can't tell them you're their uncle!"

Richard engulfed her hands in his, as if to absorb her anguish. "It's not important what they think I am as long as I become part of their lives." Richard looked at her, no doubt correlating how the same applied to Mauri. Turning his gaze back to the distraught Rose, his lips crooked in a smile. "Tell them I was your dearest friend when you first got adopted. They'll end up calling me uncle anyway."

Just as tremulous relief dried Rose's tears, Isabella's mother and Amelia came back with the kids for the second time. Richard suggested they all adjourn to his place for the rest of the evening. Everyone agreed with utmost enthusiasm, Rose and Jeffrey's kids squealing in delight when Mauri told them he had a pool in his apartment.

As they all headed for their cars, Isabella hung back, looking at Richard. This lone predator who was now suddenly covered in family. And appearing to delight in them as they did in him.

Only she felt like the odd woman out. As she was.

If he no longer wanted her, and it was clear he didn't, she'd always be left out in the cold.

Over the next few weeks it seemed as if an extended family had mushroomed around Isabella's immediate one. Rose's adoptive family, Richard's friend Rafael and his wife, Eliana—the recipe fairy, as she'd come to be known in their household—and Isabella's own siblings. With the latter now living abroad, two in France and one in Holland, they'd all come to visit on her return to the United States and were delighted with her new status quo.

She was the one who suffered more the better things got.

Not that she felt alienated by everyone's focus on Richard. *That* pleased her, for him, and for everyone else. It was Richard's distance from her that was killing her inch by inch every day.

Today, as with every Saturday, Richard was coming to take them to spend the day with everyone who could make it. He'd been taking them on outings that only a man of his imagination and influence could come up with and afford. She'd cautioned him he'd been overdoing it, building unrealistic expectations that he'd always be that available, that accommodating.

His answer had shaken her, since it was the very reason she wanted to make every second with Mauri count. He said that Mauri would be seven only once, that soon he wouldn't think it cool to hang around with him or be as impressed or as easily pleased by him. But he had another reason she didn't. He had seven years of absence to make up for.

He'd ended the discussion by reassuring her that Mauri understood he might not be able to keep up this level of presence, that he'd managed to clear his calendar to spend this time with them, but that that might not always be the rule.

Then she'd tried to call him out on his extravagance. Though his trips were fun and enriching for all of them, they cost a ton. He'd waved her concern away. He already owned the transportation and commanded most of the personnel and services involved. He'd insisted she sit back and enjoy someone doing things for her for a change.

She would have enjoyed the hell out of it, had it been meant for her. Or even partially for her. But she was incidental to him as Mauri's mother. And she could no longer take it. If he wanted to be with his son, he should be, without dragging her along.

Decision made to tell him this today, she rushed to hide the signs of her tears when she heard the bell ring. He was already here.

Mauri stampeded down the stairs to open the door to the man he now lived to anticipate.

Tears welling again, she listened to the usual commotion of father and son meeting. This time it was even more enthusiastic, as if it was after a long absence when they'd seen each other forty-eight hours ago. Yesterday was the first time in weeks Richard hadn't spent the evening with them.

When she brought herself under control, she walked down to excuse herself from their planned outing. Both of them would probably welcome that, must be unable to wait to be alone together.

Before she took the turn into the living room, she froze.

Mauri's voice carried to her, serious, almost agitated.

"Do you know that my real name is Ricardo? Today I discovered it's Spanish for Richard. Mom used to call me Rico until I was two, then started calling me Mauri. But I always hated Mauri. I always wanted to be Rico."

Slumping against the wall, tears stung her eyes again. She hadn't even realized that Mauri—Rico—remembered. What had she done to her own son to ameliorate her own suffering?

There was absolute silence. Richard, for the first time, had no ready answer.

So Mauri…Rico just hit him with his next question.

"You're my father, right?"

That question had come much later than she'd anticipated. Her knees still almost gave at finally hearing it.

Every nerve quivered as she waited for Richard's answer.

By now she knew anything she'd ever feared on Mauri's…*Rico's* behalf would never come to pass. Richard, for all his darkness and complexities, was proving to be a better father to Rico than she could have ever wished for. He was beyond amazing with him. She believed he either loved their son or felt all he was capable of feeling for him. Rico would be safe and cherished with him. And Richard had revealed himself to be a tremendous role model, too.

Powerful, resolute, committed, brilliant, everything a boy could look up to and wish to emulate. Not to mention that she didn't think Rico could go back to a life without him.

What she feared now was all on her own behalf.

If Richard revealed the truth and demanded to be in his son's life indefinitely, she could only continue to do what she'd been doing. Make his presence in their lives as welcome as could be. She wanted Rico to have his father.

But his desire for her had come to an abrupt end the moment she'd gone from black widow in his eyes to hardworking doctor and the steadfast mother of his child.

She could have lived with that, if only she didn't yearn for him. More than ever. For against all her efforts and better judgment, what she felt for him made her previous emotions fade into nothing. If she'd loved him before, she worshipped him now, while he'd never felt anything beyond desire for her. A desire that had ceased to exist.

But she might have been able to put up with seeing him regularly, as she'd been doing so far, even knowing he'd rather she wasn't part of the equation. What made it untenable was the thought that he might, probably would, one day find the one woman for him, fall head over heels in love with her as his friends had with their wives and marry her.

How could she survive watching him with another woman up close for the rest of her life, the life she knew she'd spend alone if she couldn't have him?

A one-note ring made her jump. She felt around in her pocket frantically before she realized it was Richard's phone.

He answered at once. "Numair?" After moments of silence, he exhaled. "Mauricio…Ricardo, I'm sorry, but I have to run. Numair, the partner I told you about, said it's an emergency. I don't know if I'll be back in time to have our outing, but we'll continue our discussion later, I promise."

Isabella stumbled away, ran into the study. Listening to him practically run out of the house, she sagged down.

She'd thought Richard would finally tell Rico the truth

and she'd start dealing with the new reality, for worse, or worst, and be done with it.

Now she had to wait. For his return.

To start a new chapter with his son.

And to close hers forever.

Ten

Richard didn't know whether to feel thankful or enraged at Numair's summons. He'd interrupted one of his life's most crucial moments.

But there was one rule they lived by in Black Castle. If one partner called, everyone dropped everything *at once* to answer.

But what would he have done if Numair's call hadn't taken precedence over even Mauricio's...Ricardo's...*Rico's* question?

He'd wanted to snatch him in his arms and tell him, "*Yes. I'm your father. And I'm never leaving your side ever again.*"

Now he'd never know if he would have.

Those past weeks with him, with Isabella, had turned him inside out. He felt raw, giddy, ecstatic, off balance. And terrified. As much as he'd once been for his family's safety.

He'd been scared of making one wrong move and shattering that unexpected perfection that had sprung between them all. He'd battered his way through every personal situation in his life, because he'd been dealing with men who thrived on adversity, equals who only got stronger with conflict. But mainly because he'd known when all was said and done, he'd mattered to no one. So nothing had really mattered.

But although he'd been in constant agony needing Isabella, he'd been unable to reach out and take her. Even if she still wanted him, he'd feared reintroducing such tempestuous passion would destroy their delicate new status quo, messing up this harmony he hadn't dreamed they could ever have.

That had only been his initial fear. He'd progressed to worse possibilities soon after. That if he pursued her, she'd let him have her again, but that intimacies would never let her see him beyond sex. Knowing the real her now, that would have never been enough. He feared she would have pushed him away sooner or later, but remained always near for Rico's sake. He had no doubt someone as magnificent as her would have eventually found someone worthy to worship her.

He didn't want to imagine what he was capable of doing if he saw her in another man's arms.

Everything inside him roiled until he reached Numair's penthouse.

The door opened before he rang the bell and, without a glance, Numair turned and left Richard to follow him inside.

A melodious voice heralded the approach of what he'd once thought an impossibility. Numair's bride.

Before she noticed his presence, Jenan clung to her husband's neck and they shared a kiss like the one he'd seen them exchange at their wedding. A confession of ever-present hunger, a pledge of ever-growing adoration.

The sight of his former friend so deliriously in love with his princess bride had been a source of contentment before. Now it tore the chasm of desolation inside him wider.

He longed to have anything even approaching this bond with Isabella. But there was no chance for that. He'd done her so many wrongs, he couldn't dare hope she'd ever forgive him, let alone love him as he loved her.

Yes, he'd long admitted the overpowering emotions he felt for her were love. Far more. Worship and dependence that staggered him with their power. He believed he'd always felt all that for her, with the events of the past weeks turning their intensity up to a maximum. He'd only spent years telling himself she was nothing to him so he could live on without her. But while he'd destroyed Burton, he'd also damaged something infinitely more vital. Isabella's budding love. Which had only been possible when she'd been oblivious of his true nature. He'd made reclaiming it far more impossible since he'd barged into her life...

"Richard, what a great surprise!"

He blinked out of his oppressive musings as Jenan strode toward him, still spry in her third trimester of pregnancy. Her hand embraced her husband's, as if they couldn't bear not connecting. She glowed with Numair's love, her body ripe with its evidence. It was literally painful to look at her.

He'd missed it all with Isabella. He hadn't been there to cherish and protect her while she'd carried their child. Instead, his actions had put her in distress and danger. If not for her strength and resourcefulness, the outcome could have been catastrophic. As it was, he'd caused her years of strife and misery, had caused Rico's premature birth. He could have caused his death, and Isabella's.

"If my presence is a surprise—" he growled his pain "—then your beloved husband neglected to tell you that he made me drop a crucial matter to answer his clearly fraudulent red alert."

Jenan pulled a leave-me-out-of-it face. "*And* that's my cue to leave you colossal predators to your favorite pastime of snapping and swiping at each other." Planting a hot kiss on her husband's neck, she murmured, "No claws or fangs, hear?"

Numair's love-filled gaze turned lethal the instant he directed it at Richard. "No promises, *ya habibati.*"

Chuckling, supremely confident in her husband's ultimate benevolence, Jenan passed Richard, dragging him down for an affectionate peck before striding out of the penthouse.

The moment she closed the door, Numair growled, "What the *hell* is the matter with you?"

"With *me*?" Richard's incredulity immediately turned to anger. "Numair, you've never caught me at a worse time—"

"Tell me about it," Numair interrupted.

"*And* it's not in your best interest to provoke me after—"

Numair talked over him again. "After I almost took a bullet for you."

Everything went still inside Richard. "What?"

"I trust you remember Milton Brockovich?"

Richard frowned, unable to even guess at the relevance of Numair's question. He had no idea how he knew of Brockovich.

Four years ago Brockovich's older brother had raped and almost killed a client's daughter. Richard had saved the girl, would have preferred to take the scum in, but he'd pulled a gun on him. So Richard had put a bullet between his eyes. He'd seen the younger unstable Brockovich in the precinct, and he'd ranted that he'd get even with him.

Richard had considered liquidating him as a preemptive measure, before dismissing him. He'd decided the airtight security measures he constantly varied would take care of Brockovich if he ever developed into an actual threat.

"And do you remember forcing me to pledge to fulfill any one demand in return for information leading to Jenan's whereabouts when she disappeared?"

"You mean when she discovered you were using her?"

Numair sneered. "I hated being indebted to you. So when Rafael told me of your domestic adventures with those suburban doctors, I knew something was wrong. I watched you, looking for an opening to do something big enough, preemptively, to fulfill my obligation to you. And I discovered you've converged massive security on those people, for no apparent reason...and neglected your own."

Richard frowned. Numair was right. His personal team did nothing without constantly updated orders. The ones he'd forgotten to give them…for weeks now. Not that this should matter. His personal security was a matter of paranoia on his side, not an actual necessity.

Numair went on. "I know you're probably one of the most unassailable men on earth, but I had a bad feeling about this. Knowing you're at your headquarters early on Saturdays, I decided to confront you. I caught up with you as you left the building—just in time to see Brockovich pull a gun on you. The Cobra I know would have sensed him a mile away. Wouldn't have let him breach that mile in the first place. You didn't even notice him as he passed you. He turned to shoot you and I was on top of him, diverting the bullet and knocking him out. You were gone by then without noticing a thing. I put him someplace where he won't cause anyone trouble again, but I got this—" he held up a bandaged forearm "—from a ricocheting piece of pavement. And I had to lie to Jenan about it."

Richard could only stare at him.

"You didn't hear the silenced gunshot or notice the commotion behind you in an almost empty street."

Richard shook his head, dazed. "You saved my life."

Numair gave a curt nod. "And since you saved mine when you reconnected me with Jenan, this repays my debt."

Unable to stand anymore, Richard sagged on the nearest horizontal surface, dropping his head in his hands.

Numair came down beside him. "What the *hell* is going on with you, Cobra?"

He slanted him a glance without raising the head that felt as if it weighed half a ton. "Don't tell me you care."

"To borrow what you said—when you helped me resolve Zafrana's debts, saving Jenan's kingdom and its king, her father—if I didn't, I wouldn't have intervened on your behalf."

"You didn't do it for me. You were just discharging your debt. You're terminally honorable that way."

"That notwithstanding, and though I might have seriously considered killing you before, I wouldn't want your life to end at the hands of such a worthless scumbag."

"You think I deserve a more significant end, eh?"

"Definitely a spectacular one." Numair's expression suddenly grew thunderous. "Will you tell me what the hell is wrong with you? Are you…sick?"

Richard's breath left him in a mirthless huff. "You can say that." Before Numair could probe, Richard sat forward, deciding to end this meeting. "Thanks for bringing this to my attention. And for saving my life. I'm in your debt now. You know the drill. You can ask for anything and it's yours."

"Again, to echo what you said to me before, I'll collect right now. Answer my questions."

"Why? Really, Phantom, what do you care?"

"Let's say now I've found this hugely undeserved bliss with Jenan, and you do have a hand in it, I can no longer hang on to my hatred of you. I don't want to. I want to wipe the slate clean, don't want to let old animosities taint the new life where our child will be born. Especially since you turned out to be human after all, apparently wanting a woman so much you've been putting up with her family and friends for weeks on end. Not to mention slipping up like mortals do. So just tell me the truth, dammit."

Richard had long thought it pointless to tell Numair why he'd betrayed him, causing him to be punished within an inch of his life for two months straight. But he wanted to stop hiding from him, as he'd stopped hiding from Rose, and from himself. He needed to resolve the issues between them, once and for all.

So he told him the truth. About everything.

To say Numair was stunned would be an understatement.

Suddenly heaving up, Numair dragged him with him by his lapels, his teeth bared, his shout like thunder. "All these years…you *crazy* bastard…you let me think you betrayed me, made us live as enemies…*all these years*."

This wasn't among the possible reactions he'd expected. Numair was enraged…but not as he'd thought he would be.

Richard swallowed the thorns that had sprouted in his throat. "I did betray you. I almost had you maimed. I did get you scarred. And it didn't matter why I did."

Shock expanding in his eyes, Numair shook him, hard. "Are you mad? Nothing else mattered. You had no other choice. Your family had to come first. You did the only thing to be done, sacrificing the one who could take the punishment for those who couldn't. I'm only damned sorry it didn't save your family. I would have taken far more damage if it had ultimately spared their lives."

Richard tore himself from Numair's furious grip, sagged again to escape the contact, the crashing guilt, the crushing futility. Numair's hands descended heavily on his shoulders.

"Look at me." He did, letting Numair see the upheaval filling his eyes. Numair winced. "I went mad all these years, hated you as fiercely as I once loved you for never giving me an explanation, not for the betrayal itself. You were the first person who ever gave me a reason to cling to my humanity, the one I looked up to, the one who gave me hope there'd one day be more for me than being The Organization's slave. Because there was more with you, a friendship that I thought would last as long as we both lived. I hated you, not because I got scarred, but because I thought you took all that, my belief in you, in our bond, the strength and stability it brought me, away from me."

Moved beyond words, Richard stared up at Numair, the stinging behind his eyes blurring his vision.

Numair sat, fervor replacing the fury on his face. "But I have my friend back now. And you have me, too. It's twenty-six freaking years too late, but better late than never. You damn self-sacrificing jackass."

Richard coughed. "That was no self-sacrifice. I just believed there was no forgiving my crimes. I only hoped you'd consider, after all I did over the past ten years, that I atoned for them, at least in part. But you're as unforgiving as your homeland's camels."

Numair arched a teasing eyebrow. "What, pray tell, did you do to atone? It was *I* who deigned to put my hand in that of my betrayer to build Black Castle Enterprises for us all."

"You deigned nothing. You couldn't do it without me."

Numair's face opened on a smile Richard hadn't seen since he'd been fourteen. "No, I couldn't. And I now believe what Rafael kept telling us all these years. That my escape plan wouldn't have worked, certainly not as perfectly as it had, without your help." Suddenly a realization dawned in Numair's eyes. "You waited until we were all out before you left, too, didn't you?"

Letting him read his answer in his eyes, Richard attempted a smile. "We didn't do too shabbily for sworn enemies, did we?"

Numair clapped him zealously on the back, imitating his accent. "We did splendidly, old chap."

The knife embedded in his chest only twisted at Numair's lightheartedness. "At least, you did. You're there for the woman you love every moment she needs you, to love and protect her. You'll share with her every up and down of childbirth and child rearing. You'll never leave her to face a merciless world alone, like I did with Isabella."

Numair frowned again. "You had reasons for your actions, and she understands them like I do now. The fact that she let you in your son's life attests to that."

"She may understand, even forgive, but she'll never forget, not what I did in the past, or what I did when I first invaded her life again. She'll never love me again."

Numair grabbed his shoulder, turning him fully to him. "When has *never* been a word in your vocabulary? You keep after something until it happens. So you lost seven years of your son's life…"

Unable to bear Numair's placation, he tore his hand off, stepping away from him. "I didn't lose them, I *threw* them away. When I didn't give her the benefit of the doubt, didn't trust my heart about her, when I left her in the hands of the monster who'd destroyed my family. I almost cost her, and Rico, their lives…"

"Stop it, Richard," Numair roared, bringing his tirade to an abrupt end. He'd never called him Richard before. "You won't serve them by wallowing in guilt. From now on, you'll live to make it up to her, and to your son. From what Rafael tells me, the boy worships you. And she's trusting you to be around him. This says a lot about her opinion of you as you are now, and of your efforts to *atone*. Keep at it, prove to her how much you love her and your son. When she realizes the best thing for her is to open her heart to you again, she will. Hang in there. When she bestows her love and trust on you again, nothing will ever touch that blessing. I know."

Richard only nodded so Numair would let this go. He couldn't bear one more word on the subject.

Satisfied that he'd talked him down, Numair let Richard divert their conversation to their own shattered relationship. Numair did more than wipe the slate clean. He pushed a re-start button where they'd left off as teenagers.

Numair finally let him go two hours later, and only one thing he'd said looped in his mind until it almost pulped it.

When she realizes the best thing for her is to open her heart to you again, she will.

What Numair thought would bolster his hope for a future with Isabella had only pulverized it, since she undoubtedly realized the best thing for her would be to never open her heart to him again, to stay as far away from him as possible.

When he finally worked up enough nerve to go back to Isabella's home, it was she who let him in. She'd sent Mauri out with Rose's family and stayed behind to talk to him.

With foreboding descending on him like a suffocating shroud, he followed her into the living room.

Once they sat, the voice he now lived to hear washed over him, a tremor traversing it.

"I overheard you and Mauri…and *Rico*…earlier today."

So she'd heard their son's desire to be called Rico again. And his demand for Richard to admit that he was his father.

Would she forbid him to do so, revoke his privilege to come to her home and spend time with Rico? Would she cast him out?

Isabella's hushed words doused his panic. "If you need my blessing to tell Rico the truth, you have it, Richard. I will accommodate your every desire to be with him."

The delight that detonated within him almost blanked out the world.

She wasn't casting him out but letting him further in. As Numair had said, she'd grown to trust him with Rico, was giving him the ultimate privilege of claiming his son.

But…was she telling him that was the extent of their relationship? He'd only be Rico's father, but…nothing to her?

In the past he'd been worse than nothing, her bane, steeping everything between them in deceit and manipulation, then in lust and degradation. If he'd intentionally set out to destroy her feelings for him, he couldn't have done a more complete job. If she wanted something real and lasting with a man, she'd look for it anywhere else but with him. She *deserved* the real thing. The best there was. And he wasn't it. He had sinned against her beyond forgiveness, was tainted beyond retrieval.

But since he was, what right did he have to Rico? Wouldn't he be better off without a father like him? It was even worse now that his turmoil over them could have gotten him killed today. What would that have done to Rico if he'd already known Richard was his father?

Why had he invaded their lives? What had he been searching for? Redemption? When he'd long known he was beyond that? Love? When he knew he didn't deserve it?

If he loved them, and he loved them far beyond anything

he'd thought possible, he had to make them happy. To keep them safe. There was only one way he could do that.

He rose, in an agony worse than when multiple bullets had torn through his flesh, looked down into Isabella's searching gaze and dealt himself a fatal injury. That of saying goodbye. Forever this time.

"Actually, I think you were right not to want me near your family. I'm glad that interruption stopped me from making an irretrievable statement, gave me time to realize it's not in Rico's best interests to have me in his life. Nor is it in Rose's and her family's. I'm sorry I forced myself into your lives and disrupted your peace, but I promise to leave all of you alone from now on. Once you tell Mauricio I'm not his father, he'll reconsider being called Rico, and there won't be any irreversible damage when I disappear from his life."

Shocked to her core, Isabella watched Richard walk away, feeling as if he was drawing her life force out with him.

Then the front door clicked shut behind him and everything holding her up snapped. She collapsed on the couch in an enervated mass.

She'd thought he'd be delighted with her blessing, had been about to follow it with a carte blanche of herself, if he'd consider her as a lover again.

She'd been ready with assurances that whether or not it worked out between them, it wouldn't impact the lifelong relationship she'd been sure he'd wanted with his son. The worst she'd thought would happen was his rejection of her, had been prepared to put up with anything, even watching him find love with another woman, so Rico would have his father, and she'd have him in her life at all.

She hadn't even factored in the possibility that within hours he'd decide he didn't want Rico, either.

There was only one explanation for this. He'd given the domestic immersion a go, and when the moment of truth had come, he'd decided he couldn't have her and Rico in his life on an ongoing basis. He didn't need them the way they both did him.

So he'd decided to walk away, thinking it the ideal time to curtail damages. Little did he know he'd been too late. Mauri was already so deeply attached she dreaded the injury the abrupt separation would cause him.

As for her, he'd damaged her eight years ago. But now...

Now he'd finished her.

On Mauri's return, she rushed to her room to postpone the confrontation until her own upheaval had settled. But he came knocking on her door, something he never did, bounding inside, asking when Richard would be coming the next day.

Sticking hot needles into her flesh would have been easier than telling him Richard wouldn't come at all.

Rico's reaction gutted her.

He wasn't upset. He was hysterical.

"He wouldn't leave me!" he screamed. "He promised me he'd come back to tell me everything. It's you who never wanted to tell him about me. You don't like him and keep silent when he's here, no matter how nice he is to you. You kept looking at him with sad eyes until you made him go away. But I won't let him go. He's my father and I know it and I'll go get him back!"

"Mauri...darling, please..."

"My name is Rico!" he screamed, and tore out of her grasp.

It was mere seconds before she realized he hadn't bolted to his room, but downstairs and out of the house. She hurtled after him, spilled outside in time to see him dart across the street. She hit the pavement the moment a car hit him.

Eleven

It was true that catastrophes happened in slow motion.

To Isabella's racing senses, the ghastly sequence as her son flew into the trajectory of that car, the shearing dissonance of its shrieking brakes, the nauseating brunt of its unyielding metal on Rico's resilient flesh and fragile bones was a study in macabre sluggishness. It had been like that when her father had been shot dead a foot away from her.

Then her son's body was hurled a dozen feet in the air, with all the random violence one would toss a scrunched piece of paper in frustration. He impacted the asphalt headfirst with a hair-raisingly dull crunch, landing on his back like one of his discarded action figures. At that point, everything hit an insane fast-forward, distorting under the explosion of horror.

She hadn't moved, not consciously, but she found herself descending on him, crashing on her knees beside him, her mind splintering.

The mother in her was babbling, blubbering, falling apart in panic. The woman whose life had been steeped in tragedy and loss looked on in fatalistic dread. The doctor stood back, centered, assessing, planning ten steps ahead.

The doctor won over, suppressing the hysterical mother under layers of training and experience and tests under fire.

From the internal cacophony and external tumult rose her mother's voice, as horrible as it had been when her husband lay dying in her arms, shouting that they were a doctor and a nurse, and for everyone to stand back. Everything stilled as she accessed the eye of the storm inside her, examined her unconscious son as detachedly as she would any critical case.

Her hands worked in tandem with her mother's as they zoomed through emergency measures, tilting his head, clearing his airway, checking his breathing and circulation. Then she directed her mother to stabilize his neck and spine, stem his bleeding while she assessed his neurological status. The ambulance arrived and she used all its resources and personnel as extensions to her hands and eyes in immobilizing, transferring and resuscitating Rico.

Then there was nothing more to do until they reached the practice. Nothing but call for reinforcements.

She knew she should call her partners. But the first call went to the only one she needed with her now.

Richard.

Even if he'd walked away, half of Rico remained his. Even if he'd chosen not to be Rico's father, he'd once told her he wanted to be her ally. Only an ally of his clout would do now.

While she was a pediatric surgeon with extensive experience in trauma, this was beyond her ability alone. Rico needed a multidisciplinary approach, with a surgeon at the helm who counted neurosurgery as a top specialty. Only one surgeon with the necessary array of capabilities came to mind. Someone only Richard could bring her.

The line opened at once and a butchered moan escaped her lips.

"Richard, I need you." This sounded wrong, was irrelevant. She tried again. "*Rico* needs you."

The moment Richard felt his phone vibrate he just knew it was Isabella. Even if the look in her eyes as he'd walked away had told him he'd never hear from her again. If he was right, and it was her calling him now, then something terrible must have happened.

Then he'd heard her voice, sounding like the end of everything. *Richard, I need you. Rico needs you.*

He listened to the rest and the world did come to an end around him.

Rico. His son. Their son. In mortal danger.

Without preliminaries, she ended the call. The worst possible scenario lodged into his brain like an ax.

No. No. *He's fine. He* will *be fine.* She'll save him. *He'll* save him. Antonio. He *must* get Antonio.

Barely coherent as he tore through traffic on his way to her, to his son...to his *family*, he called Antonio. He was Black Castle's resident omnicapable medical genius, who'd saved each member of the brotherhood, except him, as he'd never been part of it, from certain death at least once. After Isabella herself, he'd trust no one else with his son's life.

As per their pact, Antonio answered at once. In his mounting panic, everything gushed out of him. Antonio calmly estimated he'd be in New York with his fully equipped mobile hospital in an hour. But if the condition was critical, they must start without him.

Richard called Isabella back, including her in a conference call so she could give Antonio her diagnosis directly, as the expert, and the one who'd been at the accident scene.

But that had been no accident. He'd done this. Every time he came near her—them, he almost destroyed them.

In a fugue of murderous self-loathing he heard Isabella give Antonio a concise, comprehensive report of Rico's injuries and her measures to save him, her voice a tenuous thread of control.

Isabella... This miracle fate had given him when he'd never deserved her, who'd given him another miracle, only for him to throw her—throw them away, time and again.

His mind fragmenting under the enormous weight of guilt and dread, he'd almost succumbed to despair when

Antonio's authoritative tone dragged him back to focus with the first ray of hope. His verdict.

"From his signs, your diagnosis of a subdural hematoma with a coup-counter-coup cerebral contusion is correct. From his vitals, your measures have stabilized him and stopped the brain swelling, which will resolve over time. But he will need surgery to drain the hematoma and cauterize the bleeders. It's not as urgent as I feared, so I can be the one to perform it. Bring him to the tarmac. I'll have the OR ready."

The terrible tension in Isabella's voice rose. "We're already at the practice, and I wouldn't move him again. Our OR is fully equipped. I'll prep him and wait for you there."

Antonio didn't argue. "Fine. I'll bring my special equipment. Continue to stabilize him until I arrive. Richard—send a helicopter to the jet."

Emerging from the well of helplessness, latching on to something useful to do, Richard pledged, "I'll get you to the OR ten minutes after you land."

Once at the practice, Rose intercepted him, restraining him from stampeding in search of Rico and Isabella.

They were in the OR, and the most she could do was take him to the lounge where surgical trainees observed surgeries, *if* he promised not to distract Isabella or to agitate her, when she was miraculously holding it together.

Ready to peel his skin off to bolster Isabella, he gave Rose his word. Once they arrived, nothing could prepare him for what he saw through the soundproof glass. It would scar his psyche forever.

Rico, looking tinier than the strappy, big-for-his-age boy he adored, lying inert and ashen on the operating table. Isabella in full surgical garb, orchestrating the team swarming around him: Jeffrey, Marta, other nurses, an anesthesiologist.

Then Isabella raised her head. The one part of her visible,

her eyes, collided with his. What he saw there before she turned back to their son almost brought him to his knees.

"He'll be fine." Rose caressed his rock-tense back, tugging him to sit on the viewing seats.

His eyes burned. "Will he?"

Assurance trembled on Rose's lips. "She already saved him from the worst at the accident scene. The surgery is necessary, but I believe the life-threatening danger is over."

A rough groan tore from him, and he dropped his head into his hands, unable to bear the agony of hope and dread.

"She's amazing, isn't she?"

Rose's deep affection made him raise his head and look down at Isabella once more. He wondered again how fate had found it fit to bless him with finding her. His only explanation was so he'd lose her, the worst punishment it could have dealt him. But that was what he deserved. Why had fate chosen to punish *her* by putting him in her path time and again?

"Look at her—functioning at top efficiency even though it's her son on that table. I don't think I would have held together in her place. But Isabella's survived and conquered so much, she channeled that strength to take on the unimaginable responsibility of Rico's life."

Realizing she'd just said Rico's name, he looked at her.

A smile of reproach quivered in her tear-filled eyes. "I almost fainted when Isabella finally told me the truth. It's why I am up here, not down there." A beat. "Not that I didn't know it from the first moment I saw you together. I kept hoping you'd tell me all this time. Why didn't you?"

"I…I…left it up to her to tell you." It hurt to talk, to breathe, to exist. And he deserved far worse, a life of constant agony. "I was on probation, and she didn't know if I'd work out. I didn't. I was a catastrophic failure. I was leaving them, leaving all of you. I'm the reason this happened. I almost ended up killing my son."

"You were leaving? God, Rex, why—?"

Rafael, Eliana, Numair and Jenan walked in, cutting off Rose's anguished exclamation.

Eliana rushed to hug him. "Antonio called us."

Rafael hugged him, too, and he saw in his eyes that Numair had told him everything. But there was no surprise there, just reaffirmed faith. Rafael had always believed in him, no matter the evidence against him.

"I called him as I walked in, and he said he'll be landing in a few minutes," Rafael said. "My helicopter is waiting beside his landing lane. He said he'll drop off with his gear outside the practice like he does on missions. I coordinated with the police so they don't pursue him or my pilot."

Numair added, "The others are on their way. Is there anything else we can do?"

Richard shook his head, choking on too many brutal emotions to count. His son lying there, his fate undecided. The love of his life doing what no mother should, fighting for her son's life. The unwavering support of Isabella's and Rose's families. All his friends rallying around him.

Yes, friends. Brothers-in-arms. Just...brothers.

And he again wondered...how he deserved to have all these people on his side when he'd done nothing but waste opportunities and make horrific decisions.

Suddenly, Antonio rushed into the OR already gowned. And as if they'd always worked together, he and Isabella took their places at the table. After Isabella filled him in as he set up his equipment and examined scans, Antonio looked up, gave Richard a nod, a promise. His son would be fine.

Isabella looked up, too, sought only his eyes, and he wanted to roar for her to leave it all to Antonio. She'd suffered enough. But he knew she'd see it through, could only be thankful his son had such a mother.

"All right, everyone..." Antonio's voice filled the lounge. "Out." Before Richard could protest, he pinned him in his uncompromising gaze. "Especially you, Richard."

Everyone rushed out immediately, but Richard stood rooted, even as Rose and Rafael tried to pull him away. He couldn't leave Rico. He *wouldn't* leave *her*.

He'd never leave either of them again.

His gaze locked with Isabella's, imploring her.

Let me stay. Let me be there for both of you.

Her nod of consent was a blessing he didn't deserve, but he swore he'd live his life striving to.

She murmured and Antonio exhaled. "Dr. Sandoval decrees that you stay. But make one move or sound and you're out." At Richard's eager nod, Antonio looked at Rose. "Sorry I kicked you out with the rest, Dr. Anderson, but I did only so you'd keep your big brother on a leash. Now you'll do it in here."

Rose's relief was palpable as she dragged him to sit down. He sank beside her, clinging to Isabella's eyes in one last embrace, trying to transfer to her his every spark of strength, pledging her every second he had left on this earth, whether she wanted it or not. She squeezed her eyes, as if confirming she'd received it all.

Then the procedure started.

Richard had been in desperate situations too many times to remember. But none had come close to dismantling him like the two heart-crushing hours before Antonio announced he was done, and they wheeled Rico to Intensive Care.

Richard found himself there, pushing past Antonio as he came out first. "I must see him."

Antonio clamped his arm. "I let you watch the surgery against my better judgment already, because Dr. Sandoval needed your presence. But if I let you back there, she'll go back, too, and I barely managed to tear her from your son's side. I don't want her around him while he's still unconscious one more second. She's been through enough."

As Richard struggled with his rabid need to touch his son,

to feel him breathe and to spare Isabella further anguish, Antonio's gaze softened as she and the others came out.

"The surgery went better than even I projected. Seems Rico has his father's armored head." Rose and his Black Castle friends who'd caught up gave drained smiles as Antonio's gaze turned to Isabella. "But seriously, Dr. Sandoval's impeccable damage control presented me with a fully stable patient." His gaze turned to Richard, hardening. "Without her, the prognosis wouldn't have been the perfect one it is now. Rico is a lucky boy to have his mom's healing powers and nerves of steel."

Another breaker of guilt crashed over Richard. He wanted to snatch Isabella in his arms, beseech her forgiveness. Only knowing she wouldn't appreciate it held him back.

Antonio extended a hand to Isabella. "It was a privilege working with someone of your skill and grace under fire, Dr. Sandoval, though I wish it wasn't under these circumstances."

Seeming to operate on autopilot, Isabella took his hand. "Isabella, please. It's me who's eternally in your debt. You were the only one I could trust my son's life with."

Antonio waved him off. "Any neurosurgeon worth his salt would have done as good a job. His condition, thankfully, didn't require my level of expertise. But it was a privilege to operate on him. He's sort of my nephew, too, you know. Whether Richard likes it or not, he's been drafted into our brotherhood."

Richard stared at him, overwhelmed all over again as everyone murmured their corroboration.

Antonio turned to Richard. "Any debt here is all yours, buddy."

Richard's nod was vigorous. "Unequivocally. I'm indebted to *everyone* here, and to the whole world, an unrepayable debt in the value of Rico's invaluable life."

Antonio chuckled, no doubt enjoying seeing Richard,

who always antagonized everyone, so ready to be every-one's eternal slave.

Richard only dragged him into a hug. He even kissed him.

Pulling back, blinking in surprise, Antonio laughed. "Whoa. Who are you, and where's the lethal and exasper-ating Richard Graves I know and love, and occasionally loathe?"

Richard exhaled. "He doesn't exist anymore."

Antonio laughed. "Nah, he's still in there. But I bet he'll never again emerge around our current company." He wig-gled an eyebrow at him. "I would have loved to squeeze you for an installment on your debt, but there'd be no fun in that when you're beyond collapse." He pulled Richard's hand, wrapped it around Isabella's. "Go get some rest."

"But…"

"But…"

Hand raised, Antonio ended their protests. "I'll hold the fort here, not that I need to. Rico is stable, but I'll keep him sedated until his brain edema totally resolves. I'd rather you don't look ninety percent dead, as you both do now, when he wakes up." He shoved them away. "Go home…now."

Twelve

All the way to Isabella's house she sat beside him, unmoving, unresponsive. Not that he'd tried to make her respond. She'd been shattered, had put herself back together so many times, he could barely breathe around her in fear that she'd finally come apart for good.

Once inside, she stopped at the living room, her eyes glazed, as if she was envisioning their evenings spent there. Without warning, a sob tore out of her, sounding as if it actually ripped things inside her to break free.

She'd held it all in until this moment. Before another thought or reaction could fire inside him, she was a weeping heap on the ground.

Crashing to his knees in front of her, he wrapped himself around her, reciting her name over and over, hugging and hugging her, as if he'd integrate her whole being into his own, or at least absorb all traces of her ordeal.

She suddenly exploded out of his arms. His heart almost ruptured. She hated his touch, couldn't bear his consolation.

But instead of pulling away, she tackled him. Stunned for seconds before relief burst inside him, he let her ram him to the ground, needing her to take her revenge, expend her rage, cause him permanent damage as he'd done to her. Hoping he'd finally atone for a measure of his crimes against her, he opened himself completely to her punishment.

She only crashed her lips over his.

Going limp with shock beneath her, he surrendered to her

as she wrenched at him with frantic, tear-soaked kisses that razed whatever remained intact inside him. Then she was tearing at his clothes, clawing at his flesh in her desperation, bathing him in her tears, her pleas choking.

"Give me...everything...I need it all...now, Richard... *now*."

That was what she needed? To lose herself in him, to ameliorate her ordeal and douse her pain?

This was an offering he didn't deserve. But it was the least of her dues. To have everything that he had. He'd give it all to her, now and forever, to do with what she would.

The barbed leash he'd been keeping on his need snapped. He completed her efforts to tear his clothes off, ripped her out of hers and surged to meld their naked bodies, squashing her against him as if he'd absorb her.

Nothing, starting with him, would ever harm her again. Or Rico. Not while he had breath left in his body.

She met his ferocity halfway, the same remembered horror reverberating in her every nuance, the same need to extinguish it driving her. She sank her teeth into his lips, whimpering for his reciprocation. Giving her what she needed, he twisted his fist in the silk of her hair, imprisoning her for his invasion. She fought him for more, urged him deeper until the stimulation of their mouth mating became distress. Tearing her lips away, she bit into his deltoid, broke his skin as she crushed herself to him. Growling his painful pleasure, the bleakness of despair shattered inside him as her unbridled passion pulsed in his arms, dueled with his, equal, undreamed of. He'd do anything...*anything*... to make it permanent.

He heaved up with her bundled in his arms. "Bed— Isabella...where's your bed?"

"No...here...I need you inside me...*now*."

Her keen sent the beast inside howling to obey her. Running to the closest horizontal surface, he lowered her there, flung himself over her even as she dragged him down. Madness burgeoned between them as she rewarded his every nip and squeeze with a fiercer cry, a harder grind of her core into his erection, a more blatant offering of herself. Her readiness scorched his senses, but it was her scream for him to *fill* her that slashed away his sanity, made him tear inside her.

He swallowed her scream, let it rip inside him as her unbearably tight flesh yielded to his shaft, sucking him into their almost impossible fit, hurling him into the firestorm of sensation he craved. The carnality, the reality, the *meaning* of being inside her again… This was everything.

And he'd always cede everything to her, the one he'd been made for.

He withdrew, his shaft gliding in the molten heat of her folds. She clung to him, demanding his return, her piercing cry harmonizing with his tortured groan.

Sanity receding further, he thrust inside her once more. She collapsed beneath him, an amalgam of agony and ecstasy slashing across her face, rippling through her body, hot passion gusting from her lungs.

"Give me all you've got… Don't hold anything back…"

Her need rode him, making him ride her harder. The scents and sounds of her pleasure intensifying, her flesh became an inferno around him, more destructive than everything he'd ever faced combined. And the one thing that made him truly live.

With every squeeze of her flesh welcoming him inside her, needing what he gave her, another fraction of the barrenness of his existence, the horrors he'd seen and perpetrated, dissipated. The poignancy, the liberation, sharpened until he bellowed, pounding into her with his full power. Crying, begging, she augmented his force, crushed herself against him as if to merge their bodies.

Knowing she was desperate for release, he sank his girth inside her to the root. She bucked so hard, inside and out it was like a high-voltage lash. It made him plunge ever deeper inside her, sending her convulsions into hyperdrive, suffocating her screams. The gush of her pleasure around his thickness razed him, the force of her orgasm squeezing his shaft until her seizure triggered his own.

His body felt as if it detonated from where he was buried deepest in her outward. Everything inside him was unleashed, scorching ecstasy shooting through his length and gushing deep inside her as if to put out the flame before it consumed them both.

At the end of the tumult, she slumped beneath him, unconscious, her face streaked in tears. He could barely hang on to his own consciousness enough to gather her and go in search of her bedroom.

Once there, he laid her on her bed, every vital piece of him that had gone missing without her back in place. She'd tell him when she woke if they were back for good, or only temporarily. If she'd bestow another chance at life, or if she'd cut it short.

Isabella felt for her phone before she opened her eyes.

Finding it on her nightstand, where she didn't remember putting it, she grabbed it in trembling hands, sagged back in a mass of tremors, tears overflowing. There were a dozen messages from her mother and Antonio throughout the night, the latest minutes ago. Rico was perfectly fine.

Before she could breathe, another blow from her memory emptied her lungs again. *Richard.*

She'd almost attacked him, made him take her…then she remembered nothing. The explosive pleasure his possession had given her had knocked her out. Afterward he'd put her in bed and…left?

Before mortification registered, a silent movement did, making her sag deeper in bed. Richard…in only pants, walking in…with a tray. The aromas of fresh-brewed coffee and hot croissants made her almost faint again. She was that hungry.

She was hungrier for him. Not that she'd jump his bones again. The overwrought situation, her excuse and what had ignited him, was over. He'd decided to walk away, and she had to tell him he was free to go. She'd be damned if she clung to him through his guilt over Rico, or any obligation to her. Being unable to stop wanting him was her curse.

Suffocating with heartache, she struggled to find words to breach the awkwardness as Richard put the tray beside her then sat on the bed. His eyes downcast under a knotted brow, he silently poured her coffee, buttered a croissant, adding her favorite raspberry jam. His heat and scent and virility deluged her, hunger a twisting serpent in her gut.

Cries bubbled inside her: that he didn't need to stick around, or coddle her, that she was okay now—*they'd* be okay. Before any escaped, he put the croissant to her lips. But it was the look in his eyes that silenced her, made her bite into the delicious flaky warmth, her senses spinning.

It felt as if he was showing her inside him for the first time. It was dark and scarred and isolated in there. A mirror image of her own insides. She'd already worked all that out, but she'd thought he'd grown so hardened, was so formidable, that his demons were just more fuel for his power, that he didn't suffer from his injuries the way she did. But he was exposing facets of himself she would have never believed existed—wounded, remorseful…vulnerable.

Enervated by the exposure, she could only eat what he fed her and drown in his gaze, in a world of aching entreaty, and what she'd despaired of seeing directed to her… tenderness.

Then he began speaking. "I've been damaged in so many ways, been guilty of so much, I can't begin to describe it. But Rico…he's purity and innocence and love personified. And you…by God, Isabella, *you*. Against all odds and in spite of all you've suffered, you are all that and everything that's shining and heroic. And while I can't breathe without you…"

That statement was so…enormous it had her pent-up misery bursting out. "B-but you didn't come near me for weeks!"

His gaze flooded with incomprehension, then incredulity. "Didn't you feel me *warring* with myself not to?"

She shook her head, every despair she'd been resigned to evaporating, bewilderment crashing in its place. *"Why?"*

"Because I spoiled everything, in every way possible. In the past and in the present. But even after I discovered the extent of my crimes against you, you still gave me another chance—but only for Rico's sake. I was going out of my mind needing you, but though I knew you wanted me still, physical intimacy had so far only driven you further away, made you despise me, and yourself. And I didn't blame you. I didn't know if I had more in me than what you already rejected. So I enforced the no-touching rule on myself to see if I could offer you what I never did, if I had something inside me that was worthy of you, of Rico…of the extended family who'd reached out and accepted me as one of their own because of you."

Every word unraveled the maze of confusion she'd been lost in, shattered the vice of anguish gripping her insides.

He'd been holding back. He still wanted her.

He went on, dissolving the last of her uncertainties, giving her far more than she'd dared dream of. "But as I fully realized the extent of my emotions for you, I started to worry about the sheer depth of my attachment to Rico, the staggering *force* of my love for you. I started to fear myself. Then Rico asked if I was his father and Numair summoned me, and it all spiraled out of control in my mind."

The staggering force *of my love for you… My love for you.*

The words revolved in her mind, spinning an all-powerful magical spell, enveloping her whole being.

Richard loved her.

As mind-blowing and life affirming as this realization

was, the more pressing matter now was his distress. The need to defuse it was her paramount concern. Her trembling hand covered his fisted one. "What happened? I could have sworn you'd come back to tell him the truth."

He continued staring at her, adrift in his own turmoil. "I was so lost in you, in my yearnings for a future together as a family, I totally dropped my guard. I almost got myself killed. And I didn't even notice it. Numair saved my life unbeknownst to me."

Each nerve in her body fired, every muscle liquefied. A wave of nausea and horror stormed through her at the idea that he could have been…been… The images were… unbearable, unsurvivable…

"That was the last straw. It made me believe that whatever I do, just because of what I am, I'd only blight your lives, cause you even more untold damages. I had to keep you safe, from myself most of all. That was why I had to walk away."

Another surge of dread smashed into her.

He believed his love, his very life, would be a source of threats to them? And that was why he'd still walk away?

His eyes were haunted, desperate, as they left hers, searched space aimlessly. "I thought my control and strength of will limitless. But it all crumbled in the face of my need for you. What can I do now when it's beyond me to leave you?"

The heart that had been pulping itself against her ribs did a full somersault. She swore.

And she did what she'd told herself she couldn't do again. She launched herself at him, over the tray, knocking everything over, tackling him down to the bed, bombarding him with kisses and raining now-ready tears all over him.

"You can do only one thing for the rest of our lives. You can love, love, *love* me, and Rico, as much as we love you."

Richard, lying speechless beneath her unrestrained passion and relief, looked as if he was coming out of a fugue.

"You *love* me?" If she'd told him she could stick to walls he wouldn't have looked more stunned. "*You* love me? How? When I did everything to deserve your loathing?"

His guilt, his hatred of himself, his conviction he didn't deserve her love felt so total, she knew he'd need a lengthy argument to persuade him otherwise. She wasn't up to that now.

She wanted to get to the good part at once. At last.

So she asked one simple question. "Do you love us? Me?"

And if she had any doubt, what came into his eyes now put it all to rest forever. It *was* staggering, the purity and totality of emotions that deluged her.

"I far more than love you. *You.* I've *always* loved you… from the first moment I saw you. But I thought you never really wanted me, and that was why you didn't come with me, never sought me again. I fought admitting my love for years, so I could move on. But I was done fighting weeks ago. I only want to worship you forever, and be the father Rico deserves, and never let you go."

Crying out, she snatched a kiss from those lips that had been the cause for her every ecstasy and agony.

"You want to know how I could love you? *That's* how. I loved you from the first moment, too. I must have *felt* your love, and it kept me bound to you, even through the misconceptions and estrangement." She melted caresses over the planes of his rugged face, sizzling in delight at the open adoration in his eyes. "And if I loved the old you with all my heart, I adore the new you that Rico unearthed, the magnificent man and human being your terrible life had buried deep within you, with all my being."

He shook his head adamantly. "Rico only melted what remained of my deep freeze, but the one who brought the whole iceberg crashing down into tiny fragments has always been you. The moment I saw you again, it was over for me." He heaved up, had her beneath him in a blink. "I want you certain of one thing. I would have admitted it sooner rather than later that I wanted nothing but to be yours, to make it all up to you, even if we didn't have Rico." His face twisted. "But we do have him, and you saved him… You saved all of us."

He buried his face in her bosom and she felt another thing she'd never thought possible. His tears.

Crying out, as if they burned her, she dragged his head up, her hands and lips trembling over his face, needing to wipe them and the pain behind them away.

No longer hiding anything from her, his emotional state or anything else inside him, he worshipped her in return. "This perfection makes me even more terrified. I don't deserve a fraction of it. How could I possibly have all this?"

After another fervent kiss, she looked into his eyes, intoxicated with the freedom of showing him everything in her heart. "You better get used to it. You have all of me forever. And Rico. And you also have Rose and her family. And my family. *And* your best friend back. Not to mention that army of partners who drafted you into their brotherhood."

His eyes turned into shimmering pools of silver. This time she knew it was with joy and gratitude.

His next words confirmed her suspicion. "It's too much."

Wrapping his massive frame in a fierce embrace, she pressed his head to her fluttering heart. "No, it isn't. You see only the bad things you did, when you had overpowering reasons…or at least was under as powerful misconceptions. But you also did so many incredible things for so many people. You sacrificed yourself for your family, then for Rafael and Numair and their—your brotherhood, then you gave Rose a second chance and watched over her all her life."

He pushed himself off her, as if unable to bear her exoneration. "But what I did to you…"

She pulled him back, never intending to let him go again. "I don't care anymore what you did when you thought I was Burton's accomplice. Neither should you." He shook his head, face gripped in self-loathing. She grabbed his face, made him look at her. "What matters is that you gave me everything."

A spectacular snort answered her claim.

It made her burst out laughing. His scowl deepened, not accepting that she should make light of it. Her lethal Cobra had turned out to be a noble knight after all.

Grinning so widely it hurt, she stabbed stinging fingers into the mane he'd let grow longer, as she loved it, which she'd been dying to do since he'd imposed the no-touching ban.

"You have," she insisted. "You've given me passion and pleasure like I never dreamed possible. And you did something else no one could have—you freed me from Burton, opened up my life to new possibilities."

"That was totally unintentional!" he protested.

She overrode his protest. "You did try to save me, and if I hadn't been so busy protecting you, I would have come with you, or I would have at least sought you, and you would have protected me." As he looked about to reject her qualifications, she tugged on his hair, stopping him. "But the greatest gift you gave me is Rico. And since your return, you've given me our own small family, and an extended one. Now you're giving me your love, this incomparable gift you've never given another."

Listening to her enumerate his countless contributions to her life, his expression softened with that tenderness she was already addicted to.

"I'm giving you *everything* I have and am. You already have it, will always have it. You can weed through the mess and extract only what you like. You can toss out the rest." Just like that, he was the uncompromising Richard Graves again.

Laughing, her heart hurting with too much love and exultation, she stormed him with kisses again. "I'm hoarding every single thing about you. I love every gnarled shred of what makes you the man I worship."

He only got more serious. "I mean it, Isabella. Just tell me everything on your mind the moment you think it, and whatever it is, it's yours, it's done or it's gone."

As he melted back to the bed, taking her with him, she luxuriated in his sculpted magnificence, her pleasure magnified unto infinity now that she knew this majestic being was hers as she was his and she'd always have the right to revel in him.

"As long as this is a two-way street and you tell me anything you want different."

"You're beyond perfect just the way you are." He looked alarmed. "Never change!"

She chuckled, delirious with his new transparency. "I guess I'll have to one day. I'll grow older."

"I already told you, you will only grow better."

"It's *you* who is growing so much better with age. There should be a law to curb your improvement." She nipped his chin, caught his groan of pleasure in hungry lips. "I constantly want to devour you."

Hunger blazing in his eyes, he pressed himself between her spreading thighs. "Devour away. I'm self-regenerating." He suddenly groaned, grimaced. "I didn't promise you the most important thing."

She wrapped her legs around his hips, pulling him back to her. "Nothing is more important than having you."

"Yes, there is. Safety. Yours, Rico's and that of everyone you love. I promise you my near-fatal slipup will never be repeated. If I feel I can't be sure of that, I'll scrap this identity and start from scratch."

Terrified all over again, she clung to him. "Oh, God, Richard, how did it happen?"

He told her and she sank back in relief. "You don't have other people who want to kill you, do you?"

"Actually, it's in everyone's best interest to keep me safe...so I can keep them safe."

"If so, what's with your security fetish?" At his rising eyebrows, she grinned. "Yes, I've noticed our security detail everywhere. I know if I'm being watched. Comes from my years in Colombia and then on the run."

He groaned, the knowledge of her ordeals something she knew would hurt him forever. "It's been a well-established paranoia since I escaped The Organization. Knowing what it would mean if they ever found out I defected, and who I am now, I'd rather always be safe than sorry."

"But you *are* generally safer than anyone on earth, barring that aberrant situation, which could have happened to anyone."

"It should have never happened to me."

"And it won't happen again, if I know anything about you. So we're not in any danger by association. What are you worried about, then?"

His lips twisted, as if she'd asked him why he breathed. "I'll *always* worry, because you and Rico are not inside my body, where I can monitor where you are at all times, and where I can keep you safe every second of every day for the rest of my life."

After another ferocious hug, she pulled back, grinned up at him. "Welcome to love. And to parenthood."

He squeezed his eyes, gritted his teeth. "It's always that bad, isn't it?"

"Far worse."

His eyes opened, blasting her to her marrow with his adoration. "I love it. I love *you*. Darling…"

Her phone rang. They froze for a heartbeat before they both lunged for it.

It was Rico. Shaking, Isabella put him on speaker. He sounded sleepy, but exactly like their perfect little boy.

"Uncle Antonio told me who he is and what happened and that he didn't expect me to wake up so soon, and that my head is as hard as my father's. You're my father, Richard, right?"

Richard covered his face with his hands for a second, dragged them down over it, his eyes filling again. "I am your father, Rico. And *Father* is what I want you to call me from now on. I'm sorry I left, but your mother and I are coming right now, and I'll tell you everything as soon as you can handle long talks. But I want you to know one thing. I'm never leaving you again. *Ever*."

Rico's squeal of delight was cut short before he slurred for them to hurry up. Antonio came on and told them to come only if they were rested, as Rico was already asleep again.

With the call over, Richard looked at her, his eyes reddened, his expression disbelieving again. "This *is* too much, my love. Too many blessings."

Overwhelmed by everything, too, Isabella clung to him. "Can you handle one more? You might have to make space inside yourself for one more person who'll love you forever." He pulled back, eyes wide in shock. She bit her lip, pulled at a patch of his chest hair. "I suspect we made another baby."

"You suspect?" he rasped, looking shell-shocked.

"Want to find out for sure?"

He exploded from her side, cursing that he'd shredded his clothes, called Murdock, told him to get him intact ones and the helicopter.

She giggled at seeing him all over the place, flustered, no doubt, for the first time in his life. "What are you *doing*?"

"I'm going to buy a pregnancy kit."

"By helicopter?"

"That's to go to Rico."

"But we're not in such a hurry anymore." He looked as if this possibility hadn't even occurred to him. "And there's a kit in the top drawer of my bathroom cabinet."

Before she finished talking, he hurtled to where she'd indicated, coming back with it in seconds.

Trembling, she rose, took it from him, her smile shaky. "I had to go to the bathroom anyway."

"Why?" Then he groaned. "Bloody hell, yes, of course, by all means. I think my mind has been irreversibly scrambled."

She planted a kiss on his chest as she passed him. "No way. But I love you even more because it's scrambled now."

Heart drumming madly, she ducked into the bathroom. In minutes, she exited, the strip held tight in her hand.

"Tell me." His voice was a ragged rumble.

She walked into his arms before she held up her fist. "I wanted to find out with you."

"Do it."

She opened her fist. The two pink lines were as clear as they had been when she'd found out she was pregnant with Rico.

On a triumphant growl, Richard crushed her to him.

Many hot tears and kisses later, Richard raised his head, scorched her to her soul with the power of his love. "I'll always live with the regret that I wasn't there for you when you were carrying Rico, that I lost the first seven years of his life." His finger on her lips silenced her protest. "But now fate has given me more than the everything it has already given me—another miracle, and a chance to fix all my mistakes. Now I get to share our new baby with you, and with Rico, from the first moment. I will be there for you, for all of you, every single second, for the rest of my life. This time, I'll do everything right."

Aching with thankfulness, she clung to him, the man she was fated for, the father of her son and of her unborn baby. "Just love me, just love us. You're all I need. All our children will ever need. If we have you, everything will always be right with the world."

Looking down at her, that god among men who loved her, he lavished hunger and tenderness and devotion on her, his every look and word a pledge. "I will live to love you. And you have me, all of me. I'm all yours, forever."

* * * * *

The door opened and there she was. He'd been prepared for a spinsterish female, a librarian type.

This woman was a surprise.

She wore black pants and a crimson blouse with a short black jacket over it. Her thick dark red hair fell in heavy waves around her shoulders. She was tall and curvy enough to make a man's mouth water. Her green eyes, not hidden behind the glasses she'd worn in her photo, were artfully enhanced and shone like sunlight in a forest. And the steady, even stare she sent Brady told him that she also had strength. Nothing hotter than a gorgeous woman with a strong sense of self. Unexpectedly, he felt a punch of desire that hit him harder than anything he'd ever experienced before.

"Brady Finn?"

"That's right. Ms. Donovan?" He stood up and waited as she crossed the room to him, her right hand outstretched. She moved with a slow, easy grace that made him think of silk sheets, moonlit nights and the soft slide of skin against skin. Damn.

"It's Aine, please."

"How was your flight?" He wanted to steer the conversation into the banal so his mind would have nothing else to torment him with.

"Lovely, thanks," she said shortly and lifted her chin a notch. "Is that what we're to talk about, then? My flight? My hotel? I wonder that you care what I think. Perhaps we could speak, instead, about the fact that twice now you've not showed the slightest interest in keeping your appointments with me."

Brady sat back, surprised at her nerve. Not many employees would risk making their new boss angry. "Twice?"

"You sent a car for me at the airport and again at the hotel. I wonder why a man who takes the trouble to fly his hotel manager halfway around the world can't be bothered to cross the street to meet her in person."

When Brady had seen her photo, he'd thought *efficient, cool, dispassionate*. Now he had to revise those thoughts entirely. There was fire here, sparking in her eyes and practically humming in the air around her.

Damned if he didn't like it.

It was more than simple desire he felt now—there was respect, as well. Which meant he was in more trouble here than he would have thought.

Need to find out just how this business venture goes?
Don't miss HAVING HER BOSS'S BABY
by USA TODAY bestselling author Maureen Child

Available August 2015

www.Harlequin.com

JUST CAN'T GET ENOUGH?

Join our social communities
and talk to us online.

You will have access to the latest
news on upcoming titles and special
promotions, but most importantly,
you can talk to other fans about your
favorite Harlequin reads.

Harlequin.com/Community

Facebook.com/HarlequinBooks

Twitter.com/HarlequinBooks

Pinterest.com/HarlequinBooks

HSOCIAL

HARLEQUIN®

A Romance FOR EVERY MOOD™

**Stay up-to-date on all your
romance-reading news with the
Harlequin Shopping Guide,
featuring bestselling authors, exciting new
miniseries, books to watch and more!**

The newest issue will be delivered right to you
with our compliments! There are 4 each year.

Signing up is easy.

EMAIL

ShoppingGuide@Harlequin.ca

WRITE TO US

HARLEQUIN BOOKS
Attention: Customer Service Department
P.O. Box 9057, Buffalo, NY 14269-9057

OR PHONE

1-800-873-8635 in the United States
1-888-343-9777 in Canada

Please allow 4-6 weeks for delivery of the first issue by mail.

THE WORLD IS BETTER WITH *Romance*

Harlequin has everything from contemporary, passionate and heartwarming to suspenseful and inspirational stories.

Whatever your mood, we have a romance just for you!

Connect with us to find your next great read, special offers and more.

f /HarlequinBooks

🐦 @HarlequinBooks

www.HarlequinBlog.com

www.Harlequin.com/Newsletters

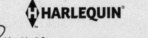

⬧ HARLEQUIN®

A *Romance* FOR EVERY MOOD™

www.Harlequin.com